CHAPTER 31

CHAPTER 31

ASHOK BHASIN

STERLING

STERLING PUBLISHERS (P) LTD.
Regd. Office: A1/256, Safdarjung Enclave, New Delhi-110029.
Cin: U22110DL1964PTC211907
Phone: +91 82877 98380/ +91 120-6251823
e-mail: mail@sterlingpublishers.in
www.sterlingpublishers.in

Chapter 31
© 2022, Ashok Bhasin
ISBN 978 93 93853 08 0

Disclaimer
This is a work of fiction. Names, characters, places and incidents are either the product of the author's imagination or are used fictitiously. Any resemblance to any actual person, living or dead, events or locales is entirely coincidental.

All rights are reserved.
No part of this publication may be reproduced, stored in a retrieval system or transmitted, in any form or by any means, mechanical, photocopying, recording or otherwise, without prior written permission of the original publisher.

Printed in India

Printed and Published by Sterling Publishers Pvt. Ltd.,
Plot No. 13, Ecotech-III, Greater Noida-201306,
Uttar Pradesh, India

PART – I

Chapter – 1

Closing the door behind her, the receptionist entered a section of the office area that had cabins one after the other. She went straight to Sanjeev Tandon's cabin. Entering, she said, 'Sir, Geetika Srinivasan has been waiting for almost two hours. Sheela Ma'am had given her an appointment at 10 a.m.'

'Have you told Sheela?' Sanjeev asked after a few seconds. He set aside the document that he had just finished reading.

'Yes, of course.'

'What did she say?' he asked, fishing out the stapler and stapling the document.

'Sheela Ma'am said I should ask her to wait.'

'You know Sheela. Quite typical of her.'

'But sir, she is *Geetika Srinivasan*, wife of the business tycoon.'

'Our Sheela Ma'am is unpredictable.'

'I know, but Geetika Srinivasan is now getting restless.'

Sanjeev thought for a while and walked to the reception area. He saw a graceful, grey-haired lady sitting there, probably in her mid-fifties. She was wearing a purple-coloured sari.

Sanjeev went up to her and politely enquired, 'Mrs Srinivasan?'

'Yes,' she replied.

'I'm Sanjeev, I'm the VP of Spellers. I'm sorry you've been waiting for such a long time. Sheela Ma'am is busy. Just a few more minutes and she'll call you.'

'If she's busy, perhaps she'd like me to come some other day.'

Chapter 31

'I don't think that'll be necessary but still, I'll ask her.'

Sanjeev returned to the office area. The first cabin on the left was Sheela Nair's, the CMD of Spellers, one of the foremost publishing houses in India. He stepped inside Sheela's cabin. She was browsing through a fashion magazine.

'Yes?' she said, looking up as he entered.

'Ma'am, Geetika Srinivasan has been waiting for a long time to meet you.'

'Yes, I know.' Sheela was unapologetic. She gestured to him to sit down. She said, 'I'm told she had sent some manuscript and wants us to publish her book.'

'That's right,' Sanjeev replied.

'What happened to the manuscript?'

'She's a new author. As usual, we rejected it and she was informed about it,' Sanjeev updated her.

'And that's why she has sought this appointment. What is the book about?'

'It's about the contribution of Indians to the IT industry.'

'How many pages?'

'Around four hundred.'

'Have you seen the manuscript?' Sheela asked, looking at him steadily.

'Yes. It seems to be a well-written book. Geetika Srinivasan is a highly educated person.'

Sheela smiled and said, 'Forget all that. Tell me, how many copies do you think we will be able to sell?'

Sanjeev kept silent.

Sheela continued, 'See, our primary business is selling. Do you expect to sell more than twenty-five thousand copies?'

'I can't give you that sort of a commitment.'

'Why don't you accept that it's not possible?'

'Yes, it isn't possible.'

'How many copies, according to you? Give me a figure, Sanjeev,' Sheela prodded.

'May be five thousand, at least initially.'

'I hope you understand that we're not running a charity.'

Sanjeev got up and was about to step out of her cabin, when Sheela called out to him, 'Okay, send her in. Once I'm through with her, you and Shankar meet me here. There is something I'd like to discuss with you both urgently.'

'Okay, ma'am.'

Sheela Nair's father had established this business years ago. Spellers gradually became a big name in the publishing industry in India, with the best retailing network. So much so that every author wanted to get their book published by them. Mrs Geetika Srinivasan was B. Tech., IIT, with an MS degree from the United States. Her husband was one of the top fifty businessmen in India. It had taken her about six months to do the research and to put pen to paper. Once satisfied with the outcome, she sent the manuscript to Spellers, with a brief note about the book and about herself but it was not accepted by Spellers. She received the usual regret note in return. She was disappointed because she had worked very hard. Mrs Srinivasan spoke with her husband, who managed to fix up an appointment with Sheela, the owner and CMD of Spellers, through a common acquaintance.

Geetika entered Sheela's cabin and after exchanging pleasantries, said, 'I had emailed my manuscript to Spellers and I received this,' placing the regret note before Sheela.

Sheela smiled, 'Yes, this is a standard note that we send to writers.'

'I understand that. I'm here to just ask you whether someone from your office really went through the manuscript. You see, I've done a lot of research and it is perhaps the best work on the subject.'

'Yes, we give equal attention to all the manuscripts that we receive,' Sheela said.

Chapter 31

Both of them knew there wasn't any truth in Sheela's statement.

Geetika smiled and said, 'I've a request. Please ask your editorial staff to go through the manuscript again. I'm sure they'll be able to find some value in the content and they can contact me if any clarification is required.'

'Sure, ma'am. I'll ask my staff to reread it. Don't worry, I'll personally monitor it. We are in the business of publishing books. We wouldn't want a good manuscript to go to any other publisher.'

'When may I call back?'

'Don't worry, we'll get back to you.' Sheela stood up, indicating that the meeting was over. She extended her hand and said, 'Leave it to me; it's my job now.'

Both smiled and shook hands, and Geetika left Sheela's cabin. Geetika wasn't completely satisfied with the meeting and was still unsure as to whether the manuscript would take the shape of a printed book.

Sanjeev and Shankar both entered Sheela's cabin for the meeting that she had termed as 'urgent'. Shankar, who was the marketing head of Spellers, and Sanjeev were the two people running the entire show.

Sheela opened a drawer and took out a book and placed it on her desk. 'Have you seen this?' She gestured at the book.

Sanjeev picked up the book and looked at the front cover. It was titled *The Grass*, written by one Ashutosh. He turned it around to read the back cover. It was a book about the movement of narcotics across the world, the mafia involved and the powerful people backing the mafia. After reading it, he handed it to Shankar.

Sheela was silently watching them. Once they were done, she asked again, 'Have you heard about it?'

Both men remained silent.

'Are you aware that this is one of the top bestsellers these days? You're in this trade. How is it that you don't know?' Sheela asked them curtly.

Shankar said, 'Yes, ma'am, I've heard about it but I didn't bother to find out more because it's not our product.'

Irritated, she demanded, 'What do you mean, it's not our product? This book has sold half a million copies all over the world! Go to any bookshop and you'll find it among the top ten bestsellers! Check the online platforms and it's selling like hot cakes. We're the best publishing company in India. This book has been written by an *Indian*. And you're saying you aren't bothered! Sanjeev, you were recommending Geetika's book to me, of which you may hardly be able to sell five thousand copies. Why can't you look at such a product? It should have been sold under our banner.'

Sanjeev listened to her tirade patiently. She was right. She was in the business for money. He was sure that Sheela would not have read a single book published by Spellers. She was never interested in the content. Her interest was only that it should sell. He asked, 'Ma'am, who is the publisher?'

'No one.'

'No one?'

'Yes, I think it's self-published.'

'But, ma'am, this is strange. A self-published book sold half a million copies! A book requires promotions, launching, reviews, marketing and whatnot. That is why people need us. How did an individual manage all this by himself? Unbelievable!'

He picked up the book again and turned to the fifth page, the copyright page of the book, which carries information about the publisher, the printer, the author and the copyright. In this book, the publisher's name wasn't there as it was self-published. The printer's name was there,

Chapter 31

so was the ISBN; and copyright to Ashutosh was mentioned. There was an email address, supposedly the author's.

Looking at them, Sheela said sternly, 'Now, go find out whether this author had sent the manuscript to us and if we sent him the usual regret note. Tell Ayesha to ask our editors if they had come across such a title or author. Get the details of all the manuscripts we've received manually or by email during the past one year. If we end up finding it, start working. I don't have to tell you what to do next.'

'Okay,' nodded Sanjeev.

'And in case it isn't there, find out the details and try to grab it. The author will not regret it. Ours is a big name. I want this book,' tapping the book, 'on our list within the next two months. How you do it, is your lookout. Do it fast, before someone else gets him, got it?'

'Sure, ma'am,' Sanjeev said.

Sanjeev and Shankar quietly left the cabin. Sheela felt exhausted. Closing her eyes, she started contemplating. It was no less than a miracle that a self-published book had managed to attract such a huge readership. While travelling last month, she had come across this book, prominently displayed in the bestselling-fiction section of an airport bookshop.

Established publishing houses like Spellers were known to not accept unsolicited manuscripts. While the standard statement included the assurance that 'all manuscripts are carefully read by the editorial staff', the truth was that they didn't even look at these manuscripts. It was well-nigh impossible for new writers to catch the attention of these top-notch publishers. Under such circumstances, literary agents became a necessary gateway for authors to enter the publishing world. A literary agent would connect the author with the publisher, negotiate the contract, talk about royalties, and assist in the sale and distribution, charging a percentage of the sales proceeds in return.

Chapter – 2

There was a long layover of about four hours at the Amsterdam airport. Rahul Mehra was returning from Chicago after spending a month with his daughter. His next flight was scheduled for New Delhi. He had no option but to spend the four hours at the airport. He walked through a long corridor and took the flight of stairs at the end of it to enter the huge lounge. On the right stood a bakery, selling all sorts of croissants, muffins, pastries, doughnuts, quiches and patties. There was a coffee shop next to it. Tired after a nine-hour-long journey, Rahul bought a cappuccino and sat down at one of the tables in the lounge. Several passengers were sitting, dozing, reading, gossiping, or just killing time.

Rahul's daughter had studied in the USA and then settled down in Chicago. His daughter kept insisting that he should stay with her as he was alone in New Delhi; his wife had expired about six years back. But he still wasn't sure if he liked the extreme cold climate of Chicago.

He looked at his watch but then realized that it was showing India time. He looked around and saw a big clock in front of him. It was quite big and a janitor was cleaning it. He was erasing the hands of the clock with a wiper and was again drawing the hands. There were no stains. Rahul couldn't understand how the person cleaning the clock could have reached or climbed up to where he was standing. Strange. He kept looking. He realized after a while that there wasn't anyone there. It was only an image of a person dressed in the uniform of the airport cleaning staff. It was mesmerizing. He saw some people making a video of the same.

He googled on his phone. It was the Schiphol clock. It was actually a twelve-hour-long recording playing on

Chapter 31

loop that created a convincing illusion that a person was standing inside the translucent clock, busy at erasing and then redrawing the hands of the clock. This timepiece was said to be the latest work of Maarten Baas, a Dutch artist.

Rahul again looked at the clock. A wonderful piece of work. How beautiful is the human brain!

He got up and saw a number of shops around him. Two shops, next to each other, caught his attention. One was a big liquor shop, the other a bookshop. Although he had been an occasional drinker at one time, he had taken to drinking regularly after his wife's demise. He went inside the liquor shop. They had a huge collection. The wine bottles were priced from €20 to 600, quite a large range. He moved around, looking at various shapes and sizes of bottles. He finally decided to buy cognac and bought two bottles. He then went to the bookshop. He had been a voracious reader since his college days. Fiction, particularly crime, murder and suspense, was his first choice. He strolled towards the rack displaying the top twenty fictions and started browsing through the books. Three of these he had finished while he was in the USA. There were books by Grisham, Patterson, Forsyth – all his favourites. Then, he saw a book titled *The Grass*; it was written by Ashutosh. A new name and that too an Indian – and available at an international bookshop! Intrigued, he read the back cover: a story on the cultivation of opium, extraction of drugs, and its movement across various countries. He looked at the brief about the author. There was no photograph; it was his debut novel. He was a postgraduate in English literature from Delhi University and was working as a lecturer in a college in New Delhi.

Rahul had a fairly good knowledge of books. Here was a young debut novelist, who had made it to the bestseller list. It wasn't easy even for an established writer to reach the top twenty bracket. He glanced through a few pages. Rahul wondered if a person with a degree in literature could be expected to have in-depth knowledge about narcotics. The writer might have a good vocabulary, a great writing style, might be able to write effective conversation, but on narcotics, well, it was quite unusual.

He knew it from his own experience.

He bought two books: *The Last Patriot* by Brad Thor and *The Grass*.

******

Sheela Nair left office at her usual time, which was around 5 p.m. Sanjeev and Shankar were sitting together in the former's cabin when Ayesha entered, carrying a tray with three coffee cups. She was the chief editor of Spellers since the last seven years. The three settled down with their coffee cups.

Ayesha smiled and said to Sanjeev, 'I heard you had an interesting meeting with Sheela.'

Sanjeev and Shankar looked at each other and grinned.

Sanjeev said, chuckling, 'Yes, very sweet. She was desperate.'

'Shankar told me about it. A perfect businesswoman!'

'She ought to be. She's the owner and not an employee like us,' Sanjeev said drily, taking a sip of his coffee.

Ayesha sipped her coffee and said, 'I've checked the mailbox. The manuscript never came to us.'

'*The Grass*?' Sanjeev asked.

'Yes. The same one. It should have been in the email. We stopped accepting hardcopy manuscripts long ago.'

'Sheela wants to have this book on our list within the next two months.'

Ayesha laughed.

'Is that an ultimatum?'

'I suppose so.'

Chapter 31

'But it's at the discretion of the author. He may refuse to get his work published by us.'

'Definitely, but everyone wants a platform like ours.'

'He's doing fine without us, you know.'

'Ayesha, could you ask your editorial staff to go through the book? Let's see what's so extraordinary about it.'

'I'm going to read it myself. In a day or two, I'll give you my feedback.'

Sitting quietly, Shankar listened to their conversation. The contents of a book or the merit of a book were not his line of expertise. He was responsible for the sales, to be in touch with distributors and follow-up regarding the quantum of inventory. And, with retail stores throughout India. He also had to keep track of books sent abroad to foreign distributors and the books being sold online, through different sites. He wasn't much aware of the manner of sale through these sites but he had two assistants working with him, who knew all about uploading book details and relevant information on these websites through their seller portal.

He addressed both of them, 'First, we have to contact the author and talk to him.'

Sanjeev said, 'Go ahead. You're a marketing man, contact him, convince him and get the manuscript. We'll publish his next edition. It shouldn't be difficult.'

'I hope so,' Shankar said.

Both Sanjeev and Shankar were depending upon the brand value of Spellers. But this would be one of the rare occasions when Spellers was reaching out to an author.

Ayesha asked, 'How will you proceed?'

Setting down his coffee cup, Shankar said, 'I've got the book here,' nodding at the book on the table. 'The author's email address is sure to be there.' He flipped open the book to the copyright page and tapped on the email address.

He continued, 'I'll send an email to this address. I hope he'll respond.'

Sanjeev said, 'Yeah, do that. Draft a nice email and fix up a meeting. I'll make myself available for the meeting.'

Looking at Sanjeev, Ayesha asked him, 'Suppose, he doesn't respond?'

'Come on, Ayesha! It won't happen. It has never happened.'

She shrugged and got up to return to her desk. Shankar too went back to his desk, and typed out the email to Ashutosh.

Dear Sir,

We, at Spellers, have seen your book 'The Grass'. It was highly appreciated by our management. Can we meet over coffee at your convenience? We may discuss about publishing the next edition of your book. If, for some reason, it is not possible for you to meet, we can email you the contract, which contains all the terms and conditions.

Looking forward to your response. You may also contact me at the number given below.

With best regards,

Shankar Prasad,

Head (Marketing),

Spellers

Like Ayesha, Shankar too was doubtful of the author replying to his email. There was no photograph on the back cover. Normally, a new author would like to be publicly known and acknowledged. He would want people to talk about him and his work. Shankar decided to call a few of his friends working in other publishing houses. A few phone calls later, he was perplexed: they were as much in the dark as he was. The manuscript hadn't been sent to anyone. That meant the author hadn't made any attempt to reach out to any publisher; he had straightaway chosen to publish the book himself.

Anyway, he thought, let's see if he responds.

Chapter - 3

At one point of time, Anand Banerjee used to work as an editor in a Mumbai-based weekly magazine. Thereafter, he worked as a freelance writer for numerous newspapers and his articles on various topics of political or social interest were published regularly by leading newspapers and tabloids. He met Sheela Nair of Spellers about four years ago at a literary festival in Jaipur. They were invited as speakers and were also interviewed by a few mediapersons. Sheela had requested him to recommend writers for her publishing house. The concept of literary agents was new in India at the time and she had learnt of the existence of such agents while travelling abroad and interacting with publishers over there. Anand initially recommended a budding writer from Bengal, after going through his work. The book was published on his recommendation and it did extremely well. When Sheela offered a commission to Anand for the recommendation, he became aware of this avenue as a source of income. He gradually drifted from being a freelancer to a literary agent. It was more rewarding, particularly because he became associated with Spellers, one of the top publishing houses.

Over months and weeks, Anand and Sheela became good friends and started moving in literary circles together. Anand didn't marry. Sheela had married but her marriage had lasted only for a couple of years. Her husband was a bureaucrat holding a senior government job. Their different lifestyle, different culture, different background and different values made them realize that they were a mismatch. They started living their individual lives separately but hadn't officially divorced. They had, on occasions, bumped into each other and behaved like old friends.

Anand owned a three-bedroom apartment, in an upscale area in Delhi NCR's Gurugram. He had converted one of the bedrooms into a study and would often work from there. He was assessing the manuscript of a new writer, a retired police commissioner who had penned his memoir. The doorbell rang. Anand knew it would be Sheela. They liked each other's temperament.

He got up and opened the door.

'Hello,' Sheela smiled her greetings as she stepped inside Anand's flat.

'Hello!' Anand hugged her and they sat in the living room.

It was a pleasant living room, though not luxurious like Sheela's. She owned a big villa in South Delhi.

'So, how was your day?' Anand asked, offering her a glass of water.

'As usual. Routine.'

'I heard Mrs Srinivasan met you today.'

'How do *you* know?' she was surprised.

'She's a big gun or, rather, wife of a big man.'

'Yeah, she met me and is rather keen that we publish her book.'

'Why don't you recommend my name to her? I'm sure she will readily dish out a handsome commission.'

'That's fine but I doubt her book will sell.'

'I'm pretty certain she herself will buy a large number of copies.'

'At a discounted price, and how many? One cannot run a publishing house that way.'

Anand smiled. He came near her and patted her shoulder, 'Cool down. Think of it as charity.'

Sheela caught his hand and snorted, 'Ask her how much charity *she* has done!'

Chapter 31

'Okay, relax. Make yourself comfortable. I'll get you your favourite drink.'

Anand went to his small bar that he was rather proud of. He poured out vodka from one of the pink-coloured crystal bottles. It read 'Alizé'.

'Your ready-made cocktail, ma'am,' he grinned as he handed it over to Sheela with a flourish.

'Thanks,' she smiled, taking it.

Anand pulled up a light chair and sat in front of her. He had always appreciated her beauty. She would be around forty-five but looked younger. She had maintained herself well and was attractively attired. Sheela was aware of the effect she had on Anand and she liked it. She had taken off her footwear and was now reclining on a sofa.

She said in mock anger, 'Don't stare like that.'

He smiled.

She took a sip and asked him, 'Have you heard about a book called *The Grass*?'

'Yes, of course. It became a bestseller within six months.'

'Have you read it?'

'Yes.'

'What's so extraordinary about it?'

'I didn't find anything special.'

'But it has attracted a huge readership, Anand. It has sold half a million copies.'

'Is that so? I didn't know that. It's strange.'

'Look, you're an expert in the literary field. You've so much experience. Surely, it has some edge over the other books?'

'To be honest, I half-read it. I didn't find it interesting; I left it midway. The language is amateurish and the plot is scattered.'

'How is it being sold then?'

'Maybe the marketing is very good?'

'Do you think our marketing is average? Anand, no one can beat our marketing and distribution. Our dealer network is very strong. Even then, none of our books has ever sold that many copies.'

'And it has been self-published.'

'You know that?'

'That's the first thing I see when I pick up a book.'

'Don't you find it odd? Bizarre?'

'Correct.'

'I've asked my staff to contact the author; I want it on our list.'

Anand laughed aloud. He got up and sat down beside her. He kissed her and said, 'You have so much money, my dear. Why bother?'

'It's curiosity, my dear. The more I think, the more curious I become. I suggest you read it cover to cover. Perhaps the climax is interesting.'

'Okay. I'll finish it now.'

Sheela had emptied her glass. He picked it up and headed to his bar to pour out another drink for her.

She said, 'Make one for yourself also.'

'Sure.'

******

Two days had passed. There was no response to the email Shankar had sent to Ashutosh's email address. He had followed it up with a reminder as well. But no one contacted him or anyone else at Spellers. Shankar had scoured Facebook and LinkedIn with the hope of finding Ashutosh. There were several profiles with the name of Ashutosh but none gave an inkling to the specific Ashutosh that he was looking for. In the last two days, he hadn't been able to find out anything about the author. He had drawn a blank at every turn. It was baffling and

Chapter 31

unexpected. Every author wanted to publicize his work and feature on social media these days.

Although his assistants had checked out Amazon and other platforms, Shankar himself went through the online sites. Sheela was correct when she'd said that the book was doing excellently: he'd observed that the book was being snapped up. Half a million copies had been sold. The printed MRP was ₹399 in India and US$12 abroad. At the current sales figure, the total revenue would come to ₹20 crore, a huge sum in the publishing industry. Shankar had been in this industry since X years. He had never seen such a stupendous sale of a book written by an Indian author. That too without the backing of any established publisher.

Ayesha came in with a copy of *The Grass*. She put the book on Shankar's desk, pulled up a chair and sat down opposite Shankar.

'Busy?' she smiled.

Shankar smiled. He asked, nodding at the book, 'Have you finished reading it?'

'Yeah, almost.'

'Your views?' Shankar asked.

'Bad. Not worth reading.'

Shankar laughed, 'Ayesha, the whole world is reading this!'

'I don't know why they are! I've gone through it, Shankar. No proper proofreading has been done; there are so many mistakes … there are errors on almost every page, be it grammar, punctuation or spelling.' Ayesha's tone expressed her exasperation.

'But the author claims to be a postgraduate in English literature.'

'Yes, you see writing a book is a different ballgame altogether. One makes innocent mistakes. Nobody teaches you punctuation or grammar at the postgraduate level.'

Shankar frowned, 'So, if no proofreading was done, it means the manuscript went into printing straightaway.'

'It looks like that.'

'But it is selling. I was searching various sites.' Shankar turned his laptop towards Ayesha.

She looked at the screen and said, 'Impressive.'

'On top of it, nobody knows who this Ashutosh is. There is no photograph nor any information on his background anywhere.'

'Do you think the sale could have been manipulated?' Ayesha asked him.

'Nonsense. Look at the copies sold online. Sheela Ma'am said the other day it is among the top ten bestsellers. My staff checked and found that the book has reached all bookshops in the city – and it's the same story in other cities. It's definitely selling.'

'Who's the distributor?'

'Not known,' Shankar shrugged helplessly.

'That you can find out surely ...'

'I'm thinking of contacting the printer. His address is given in the book.'

'Do you know the printer?'

'No, never heard of him,' Shankar said wearily.

'You mean it wasn't digital printing but offset printing.'

Shankar picked up the book, and opened it, examining the paper quality and the printing. Though it was difficult to distinguish between digital printing and offset printing, Shankar had sufficient experience to tell. He took his time in scrutinizing the book before rattling off his observations.

'This has been printed at an offset press. Good quality printing. Paper is 90 gsm. We normally use 70 gsm paper because 90 gsm paper makes the book heavy, but here the quality of paper is so good that despite using 90 gsm paper,

Chapter 31

the book isn't heavy. It is yellowish paper with a brown tint. The best quality, according to me. The paper must have been imported because I'm not aware of any manufacturer in India producing this quality of paper.'

'Maybe the book has been printed abroad and the copies are being imported?'

'The printer's address is of New Delhi. Somewhere in Okhla Industrial Area.'

'But does it matter?'

'No. Our job is to locate the author. By the way, he hasn't responded to my email.'

'Oh,' Ayesha was surprised.

'Yeah,' Shankar pursed his lips. 'I'll have to check with the printer now. That's the only lead.'

'I can suggest one more thing.'

'What?'

'There must have been reviews in different newspapers. You know everyone. They can tell you.'

'Do you think the media would have covered the book? They're all so mean. You know that. They have to be invited. You have to prepare different reviews yourself and hand these over to them for printing in their respective newspaper. They're all parasites,' Shankar paused to take a breath. 'Let me check, if there were reviews.' He scanned some online sites and came across various reviews. These were about five months old.

'You're right, Ayesha. There are reviews.'

'Now these people will tell you who organized the event, who invited them for dinner and who handed over the reviews for publishing.'

'Great, thanks!' he smiled, feeling somewhat relieved.

'Anytime,' Ayesha smiled and left.

Chapter – 4

Rahul Mehra lived in a four-storey building in central Delhi. Each floor in the building had two apartments. Rahul owned a two-bedroom apartment on the first floor; the other apartment on the same floor was unoccupied. The building was located in a busy market area. There were a lot of eateries around and all were flourishing chiefly because of a university nearby. Most of the apartments in the area were rented by outstation students.

It was a Friday night. Sitting on his bed and partially covered by a quilt, Rahul was sipping his cognac. The television was on and he was watching an English news channel, which was primarily covering the campaigns for the US presidential elections.

Rahul had never understood the complete election process that was followed in the US. It was very complicated and unlike the election system in India. He had once asked his daughter but the entire activity from the nomination till the counting stage was quite complex for him. What he could follow was that there were two main political parties, Democrats and Republicans, of which the former were considered to be liberal while the latter, the Republicans, were said to be conservatives. Different candidates within the respective party compete with each other and finally one candidate is nominated from each party, who then runs their campaign state-wise. The elections are held on the Tuesday falling immediately after the first Monday in the month of November and the president-elect is sworn in on 20 January of the following year. This much he knew.

This time, the two contenders were, Paul Johnson, a Republican, and Sarah Baker, a Democrat. The newsreader

Chapter 31

was talking about both candidates. Sarah Baker was an academician, who entered politics about fifteen years ago and gradually became popular for her liberal views on many policies on the economy, migration and armaments. The Democrats found her a suitable candidate. Paul Johnson was a rich businessman and owned a chain of hotels, not only in the US but in other countries too. He also owned a chain of retail stores in almost every city. He used to be a member of the Democratic Party but later switched loyalties to the Republican Party. The newsreader was talking about how Paul Johnson had spent a lot of money on the election campaign and that by all predictions, there was a possibility of his becoming the next president of the USA.

Rahul kept sipping his cognac as he looked at Paul Johnson's photograph that was being displayed on the screen. He narrowed his eyes and stared at Paul's face. He wondered whether this man was capable of running a country like the USA. While he was in the USA, he happened to listen to the speeches of both these people. Sarah Baker appeared to be the perfect choice, but again, it was a money game. He remembered the phrase, 'money makes the mare go'. The world was like that.

He changed the channel.

******

They were sitting in the coffee shop of The Imperial. Kalyani Nath was a journalist working for a leading Delhi-based newspaper, and she covered all literary events. Shankar had spoken with her and fixed up the meeting. She had asked him to meet at the hotel's coffee shop. The coffee here was excellent but pretty expensive as this was one of the top-notch hotels of Delhi. Nevertheless, despite the pricing, patrons would often ask for another round of coffee.

Once they had exchanged pleasantries and Kalyani had settled down, Shankar placed their order of two coffees and two savouries when the waiter quietly materialized at their table. When he departed, Shankar turned to Kalyani, 'So, how are things?'

'All fine, what about you? How is your Sheela Ma'am?' she chuckled as she asked him, raising an eyebrow.

'Sheela Ma'am is perfect, as usual.'

'Is she a regular with Anand?'

'What do you mean "regular"?'

Kalyani laughed loudly this time.

'Come on, everybody knows! They're seen together at all events, parties, dinners, etc.'

'They're very good friends,' Shankar replied.

'Let's see how long it lasts.'

'I've been seeing them together for the last four years. He's our literary agent, you know.'

'I know, I know.'

'He just cannot be compared with Sheela. She's rich ... very rich ... and Anand leads a good life but as far as I know his income is average.'

'Yeah,' Kalyani shrugged, 'or maybe a little more than average.'

Shankar paused as the waiter served them their order and continued once he had retreated.

'Tell me one thing, Kalyani. You're a woman. What does a woman look for in a man?'

She smiled and took a sip of her coffee, before replying. Shankar too picked up his coffee.

'A woman of her status would want to dominate. She would dominate even at the cost of her married life. Look, Sheela was married to a pleasant, highly educated and powerful person. I'm using the word "powerful" because he holds a senior position in a government department.

Chapter 31

Sheela couldn't dominate him. She wanted to live on her terms.'

'But there's nothing wrong if a woman wants to live on her terms.'

'Nothing. But allow the other person the same status, yes?'

Shankar put down his coffee cup, picked up the savoury and glanced around. Almost all the chairs were occupied. Between mouthfuls, he asked, 'There is a book, *The Grass*. Have you read it?'

Kalyani placed the remaining savoury on a plate and daintily took a bite before asking, 'Is Sheela interested?'

'How did you guess?' Shankar was surprised.

Kalyani laughed heartily, 'She must have got wind of it doing exceedingly well! Any book selling like that and not on the Spellers' list would be her main worry.'

'Kalyani, I read your reviews about the book. These were on the net.'

'Did you like the book?' Kalyani responded with a question.

'To be frank, I haven't read the book. Ayesha has and her view was that it isn't worth reading. But your reviews tell another story.'

'So, Spellers is reading books published by others,' Kalyani's slight taunt didn't escape Shankar.

Shankar looked at her and asked, 'Have you met the author?'

'No.'

'How can that be, Kalyani? The book must have been formally launched. You would have been invited. Drinks, dinner … the works … Was Ashutosh not present?'

'No,' she shook her head. 'It was organized by some event management company. We were given a copy of the book and the reviews.'

'Reviews were prepared by them?'

'You know all that, Shankar. You're not new to the trade.'

'Was it lavish?'

'What?'

'The event. Was it lavish?' he repeated.

'Yeah, it was held here, in the Imperial.'

'This is an expensive place.'

'Definitely.'

'Soon after the event, the book probably didn't capture the market. Whosoever he is, he has spent a lot, even before it was sold,' Shankar persisted.

'It's a promotion; it's an investment. But why are you so interested?'

'I told you, Kalyani,' impatience crept into Shankar's voice. 'In a meeting a few days back, Sheela insisted that we contact the author and bring the book on the Spellers' list. After that, I sent an email to the address given in the book. No response. Checked the social sites. No author with the name Ashutosh could be traced. There's no photograph on the book cover. I thought I must find out from you whether you've met the author. You haven't. Don't you think all this is baffling?'

Kalyani was thinking. She had never attempted to contact the author. In fact, journalists like her, routinely, never contacted them. It was the other way round. An author needed a promotion. It was always in their interest. This case really was intriguing.

'You're right. It *is* unusual.'

'According to you, a lot of money was spent at the launch event for promotion,' Shankar continued.

'Yes.'

'It's a self-published book; there's no publisher backing him. If a publisher *organizes* the book launch, it's

Chapter 31

understandable. If a publisher *prepares* the reviews for distribution to the media, it's understandable. I'm sure there's someone putting in the moolah for promoting this book!'

'You may be right, Shankar. You've made me curious too.'

'Kalyani, you have such vast experience. You've been covering events for a long time. You've written numerous reviews for numerous books. Tell me, have you ever seen a book sell *so fast*?'

'No. And now you've also told me that the book isn't worth reading. I'll have to read it now.'

Shankar laughed and said, 'That's why I say, you people should actually read the book before giving the reviews! Don't always go by what is distributed. You just consider the money given to you. You've no idea of what you are promoting. With *The Grass*, you've promoted a mediocre book!'

'Don't talk like that. It's an insult,' Kalyani scowled.

'I'm sorry. I never intended to insult you or any other journalist. But sometimes such things do happen.'

Kalyani was silent for a few minutes and then said, 'If I summarize all that you've said, it means that the author isn't interested in publicity. He's not coming forward; nor is he responding to a publisher like Spellers. Yet, a good amount of money is being spent on promotion and marketing.'

'Yes, and perhaps you haven't seen the book's review on various shopping sites. These reviews are in thousands, maybe lakhs, and everyone is praising it to glory! I'm fairly sure all these reviews have been phrased carefully, and only to promote the book.'

'Are you sure that the book is actually selling?'

'Yes. I've checked and verified that. It's being purchased.'

'Interesting.'

'By the way, who were the event managers?'

'That's not of much significance because it was organized by a media buying house.'

'Really?'

'Yes, we were invited by that media buying house. You know, they sign a contract with the client that all print or electronic media would cover the event and it would be covered according to their wishes.'

'And the media acts accordingly?'

'They're bought. They've a price. We're employees; we're instructed to attend the event and cover it.'

Shankar sighed and said almost wistfully, 'Sometimes, I wish I was in the media. They've a price tag.'

Kalyani and Shankar chatted for some time more on the current economic scenario before wrapping up their meeting. They stood up, shook hands and assuring each other they'd update one another if they hear anything definite about Ashutosh, they parted ways.

Chapter – 5

The entry to the building was from the rear. There was another commercial office on the front. Harish Pandey, the owner of Naveen Printers, parked his car in the back lane and entered his office. His office consisted of a small cabin in the right corner of a largish hall while the rest of the space had rolls of paper dumped in a haphazard manner. The printing press was installed on one side of the first floor, and the remaining half was used for storing printed and bound books. Harish had been running the press for more than ten years. Earlier, his business was going very well but with the advancement of technology, an era of digital printing came, which was quick, convenient, handy and a win-win situation for all parties concerned.

Harish was at his desk, checking some account statements, when there was a knock on his cabin door. He looked up at the unexpected and unscheduled visitor.

'Yes, please?' Harish asked.

'Naveen Printers?'

'Yes.'

The man came in and introduced himself, 'I'm Shankar from Spellers.' He took out his business card and handed it to Harish.

'Hello, I'm Harish Pandey, the owner.' He took the visiting card and glanced at it once; he requested Shankar to be seated. It was a pleasant surprise for Harish. Spellers was a big name. An executive from Spellers had come to his office to see him! Had Spellers called him, he would have rushed to their office. 'What a surprise!' he said, looking at Shankar with great interest. 'Sir, what will you have? Tea or coffee?'

'No, no. I've just had my breakfast, thank you.'

'Sir, what can I do for you?' Harish was puzzled.

Shankar took out *The Grass* from his bag and placed it before him. 'Looks like this book was printed by you.'

Harish smiled and said, 'Yes, sir.'

'The book is doing good business.'

'Yes, sir. Definitely.'

'We've been trying to contact the author and he hasn't responded to the email we sent to the address given in the book. I thought, you may be in a position to give us his contact number.'

'Is that so? But that is the address.'

'Do you have his mobile phone number, landline or his residential address?'

Harish looked at him intently. Spellers was trying to find Ashutosh. He laughed, 'Since when has Spellers started going after a writer? It should have been the other way round.'

Shankar had no answer, so he kept silent.

Harish asked, 'Is Spellers interested in publishing this book?'

'That may happen in the future,' Shankar replied guardedly.

'But it is already selling.'

'Yes, we know. Are you doing all the printing for him?'

'No, two thousand copies in one go and another two thousand in the reprint.'

'Only four thousand?' Shankar couldn't believe he heard right. 'But lakhs of copies are being sold and printed in your name.'

'I know. After the first four thousand copies, the author told me that they might engage some other printer.'

'Didn't you object?'

Chapter 31

'There's no law forbidding him to go to anyone else,' Harish leant back in his chair, trying to size up Shankar.

'But in that case, your name shouldn't be there,' Shankar immediately pointed out.

'Yes, but for some reason, he continued printing my name and address.'

'And you have no problem with that?'

Harish laughed, 'Why should there be any problem? My firm's name is being printed. Look, you're here. That's evidence.'

Shankar mulled over what Harish had just said; the printer might be right. After a brief pause, he asked him, 'Who approached you to print this book?'

'Ashutosh.'

'The writer himself?'

'Yes, he came with the manuscript and the cover design. Everything was ready. I was only to print.'

'The ISBN?'

'He had already obtained it.'

'And the paper? The paper is of very high quality – 90 gsm and still light weight.' Shankar looked around at the rolls of paper lying around. He asked curiously, 'Do you normally use this type of paper?'

'No, sir. I mostly print textbooks for schoolchildren. The paper used in these books is different,' Harish gestured at the rolls.

'Yes, I know.'

'For this particular book, the author wanted this specific paper. I contacted various importers and with great deal of difficulty I was able to procure the necessary amount of paper, which matched his requirement.'

'There is no photograph of Ashutosh,' Shankar remarked, tapping the book. 'Was he not interested?'

'I don't know. You see, printing a novel is not in my line of regular work. A textbook doesn't carry the author's photograph, so I never asked him.'

'He himself made the payment?'

'Yes, sir. Cash.'

'If you don't mind, can you tell me the amount you charged for two thousand copies?'

'Sir, you are big people. You're in this trade. You know better than me. For me, it was a one-time job,' Harish said.

Seeing he wasn't making much headway, Shankar got up and said, 'Well, thank you for your time. I have to somehow get in touch with Ashutosh. Can you help me?'

Harish stood up as well, and as they shook hands, he said, 'Sir, I've told you whatever I knew.'

Shankar was about to leave when Harish said hopefully, 'Sir, you can always consider my firm, sometimes at least, for printing your books.'

Shankar nodded, 'Definitely, I'll keep you in mind,' and left.

When the receptionist saw Shankar entering the office, she informed him that Sanjeev was sitting with Sheela and they had left a message that he was to join them. Shankar went to his desk, placed his bag and lunch box on it and headed to Sheela's cabin.

When he knocked on the glass door of Sheela's cabin, Sheela and Sanjeev were in deep conversation about *The Grass*. Shankar had briefed Sanjeev the previous evening before leaving for his meeting with Kalyani.

'Come in, Shankar,' Sheela said.

'Good morning, ma'am.'

'Yes, good morning. Sanjeev was telling me that Ashutosh couldn't be contacted,' Sheela came directly to the point, and gestured him to sit.

Chapter 31

'Yes, ma'am. Yesterday I met Kalyani Nath,' Shankar replied as he sat down.

'The journalist?'

'Yes,' Shankar replied. He then narrated their conversation. He told Sheela that an event had been held by a media buying house and the author had not been seen. Reviews had been circulated, which were ultimately printed in respective newspapers. He also told Sheela about his meeting with Harish Pandey, the printer, and brought her up-to-date with the details of his meeting. The email address that was given in the book was the only address that the printer knew about Ashutosh.

'In a nutshell, we've reached nowhere,' Sheela said grimly.

'Not exactly. We do know that somebody is investing a substantial amount of money for the promotion and marketing of the book,' said Shankar.

'Anand was telling me that the book isn't that good. He finished the book yesterday and said that it's a badly drafted book.'

'Ayesha said the same thing.'

'And yet he has been able to reach that level,' Sheela frowned.

Sanjeev said, 'Money, ma'am, money. From the looks of it, Ashutosh isn't interested in earning. He might have spent more than the revenue he has earned.'

'All this just to make his book famous?'

Sanjeev shrugged his shoulders.

Sheela mulled over it and then said, 'Shankar, can you contact the authorities and check who allotted the ISBN because it's mandatory to submit an address proof either of the publisher or of the author. In this case, there's no publisher. That means Ashutosh's address proof would be there in the office of the ISBN-allotting authority.'

'But, it's difficult to get the details from there.'

'Yes, yes. We all know,' Sheela said impatiently, 'but if one has contacts, an address can be obtained.'

Sanjeev and Shankar looked at each other. She was right.

'I'll try,' Sanjeev assured her.

'So, based on what the printer said, he had printed four thousand copies.'

'Yes, the payments were made in cash.'

'That means, the book is being printed elsewhere. Can we find out?' she asked, looking from one to the other.

'I've tried …' Shankar trailed off.

Sanjeev chipped in, 'Ma'am, perhaps you can ask Anand Sir. He's in touch with all distributors as well as book importers. There's a possibility that it may be printed abroad and distributed from there. Some quantity comes to India for retail stores.'

'I'll talk to Anand. It may not be difficult. I hope you guys get the address.'

At that point of time, the door opened and Ayesha entered. She said, 'Ma'am, I've some news.'

They all looked at her expectantly.

Ayesha said, 'The manuscript is with Scholars.'

Scholars was a subsidiary of Spellers.

'What?' they all exclaimed in unison.

'Yes. It was a shot in the dark actually. I checked the manuscripts received at Scholars, and I found it. Ashutosh had sent the manuscript for publishing – about eight months back.'

'Then, what happened?' Sheela was astounded.

'The usual. Scholars sent an email, informing him of the publishing charges – ₹1,75,000 plus taxes. He didn't respond. Scholars sent a reminder. Again, no response. Another proposal was sent to him that instead of paying

Chapter 31

the full amount in advance, he could pay fifty per cent in advance. But again, no reply.'

Shankar asked hopefully, 'Any phone numbers?'

'No, only the email address from where the manuscript was emailed.'

'Is it the one printed on the book?'

'No, it's different.'

'Perhaps we can reach him on this email address?' Shankar sounded excited.

'I've already tried,' Ayesha smiled at him apologetically. 'There was a message of delivery failure. It doesn't seem to exist at present.'

'So, he made an attempt. Not at Spellers but at Scholars,' Sheela said.

'That means, he hadn't any money to pay,' observed Sanjeev.

'At that time,' Ayesha said, smiling.

Sanjeev and Shankar got up, as Sheela turned to Ayesha, 'Can you forward the manuscript to me?'

'Sure.'

Sanjeev, Shankar and Ayesha came out of Sheela's cabin.

In the last few years, websites promoting self-publishing in a friendly, guided manner had become popular. Looking at the popularity, established publishers all over the world had prepared such sites as an alternative for new writers. Such sites gave a range of packages and each package specified the services it provided. These services included cover designing, ISBN, proofreading, editing, author's webpage, launching, promoting, distribution on book websites and at retail stores. A writer could choose some or all of these services. The books were to be printed on demand.

Scholars had listed its packages on its website. One was priced at ₹75,000, the second at ₹1,75,000 and the third at ₹2,75,000. The usual practice was to suggest the middle package to the writer. The money was usually taken in advance. Publishers normally provided fifteen or twenty copies to the author. New authors were attracted to Scholars once they came to know that it was an imprint of Spellers.

******

Ashutosh had sent the manuscript to Scholars and had then shifted to silent mode.

Chapter - 6

Normally, he prepared his own meals as he enjoyed experimenting with different ingredients in his own kitchen. But somehow, that day, Rahul Mehra didn't feel like cooking. For lunch, he went to the Chinese restaurant he preferred and ordered fried rice and veggie balls in gravy. Both the orders were served to him in fifteen minutes. While eating, he looked around. It was a noisy place. There were young boys and girls studying nearby. He saw them talking, eating, laughing, teasing and squabbling. He found some of them disputing over payments, and then contributing to the bill. Rahul smiled slightly to himself. College days were good, and students were students; their disputes were innocuous, their minds were not polluted. When they completed their formal education and went to respective professions or jobs, gradually, the cunningness, the crookedness and the greed crept in. By the time they reached middle age, there was no scope left for further corruption.

He found himself thinking how wonderful were these college days of one's life, untouched by the outside world. He enormously enjoyed and appreciated the energy of these young boys and girls.

He finished his lunch and returned to his apartment. He picked up *The Grass* that day. He had so far not started reading it. He came to the balcony and sat down. The warmth of the full sun felt good in winter. He opened the book to the first chapter.

******

It was lunchtime and Kalyani was talking to her colleague Meeta. She told her the conversation she had had with

Shankar about *The Grass*. Meeta was an investigative journalist, and she listened carefully.

'You mean, the author has so far not surfaced but a lot of money is being spent on promotion?' Meeta asked.

'Yes, and nobody knows who is spending. As a routine, we went to the event, covered the event and gave our reviews in the newspaper.'

'It didn't strike you as strange that the author wasn't present at the event?'

'It did, Meeta. But this does happen at times. There have been instances in the past when an author wasn't present at their own book launch.'

Meeta reflected for awhile on what Kalyani had said earlier and said, 'You're right. It looks unusual that a person is spending money to popularize his book to the extent that it has become one of the bestsellers, yet he's avoiding publicity. It goes against basic human nature. By this time, he should have been on every news channel and at social events.'

'Hmm,' Kalyani concurred, and then, as a thought struck her, asked hesitantly 'Is it possible that Ashutosh's name is being used and there's somebody else, behind the scene, who is interested in selling the book?'

'Maybe,' replied Meeta thoughtfully.

'Then, what's important is the person who is spending the money and who is trying to popularize the book.'

'There's one more aspect. If, by your version, half a million copies have already been sold, the total revenue would be ₹20 crore. We're not deducting discounts, etc., which is normally extended on products sold online. Out of these, four to five crores would be the cost of printing. Add to it another four to five crores as the cost of distribution worldwide. Maybe more. Further, if the person is managing all the reviews at all sites and other media, add the money so spent. Add the money on promotion, packing, delivery charges, etc. This shows

Chapter 31

that the person is apparently not in the game for earning. His only aim seems to be that the book should be read by as many people as possible,' Meeta said.

'You're right,' said Kalyani. 'But what could be the aim, the purpose? I've been told the book is otherwise mediocre.'

Meeta whispered to Kalyani, 'Forget it. The world is full of idiots!'

Kalyani chuckled and said, 'Meeta, women like you love idiots.'

'Yes, I do because to follow them is my bread and butter,' Meeta sighed ruefully.

Smiling, they got up and went back to their respective desks.

******

Sanjeev took Ashutosh's address from the ISBN authority, and passed it on to Shankar, who then had it verified. One person named Ashutosh used to live at that address along with his wife, about six to seven months ago. From the neighbours, it could be gathered that they had shifted to some other house near North Delhi Campus as both of them were lecturers at the university. This information confirmed two things. One, Ashutosh did genuinely exist and, two, he was a lecturer, as mentioned on the back cover of the book.

******

The book was about a drug mafia running the clandestine purchase and sale of opium, morphine, heroine and other synthetic drugs. Despite all these items being banned, the business was run by a Mumbai-based ringleader. He was involved in both importing and exporting the goods or, in other words, *smuggling* the goods. Synthetic drugs, particularly Fentanyl, was exported to the USA and European countries in large quantities. Opium was cultivated on large tracts of land in Latin America and Afghanistan, and it was cultivated illegally.

Based on rough estimates, billions of US dollars were involved. The calculation was simple: the price of one micro million gram of Fentanyl was half a US dollar in the international market. One could imagine the amount of money involved.

Rahul had read ten chapters. There was nothing new; all details about drugs were available on Wikipedia. The author would have gathered the information from there. Additionally, the storyline was developing slowly.

The author was an amateur. His English was good but the plot was weak. The details on opium cultivation, its extraction process from the first to final stages were exhaustive but the workings of a drug mafia appeared to be borrowed from various movies or web series, like *Narcos* on Netflix. The officers of the Narcotics Control Bureau (NCB) were developing intelligence and zeroing in on one person. They were maintaining surveillance and at the last moment, the consignment delivery was deferred. The concerned person became suspicious of a possible strike by the NCB. The mastermind had contacts within political parties and bureaucratic circles. He also had in-depth knowledge on how the various narcotic enforcement agencies functioned in all those countries where he supplied drugs. He was cautious enough to have never been caught.

That was the gist of the story up to the first ten chapters. Rahul was far from impressed. He kept the book aside and felt sad. The younger generation wouldn't know of the consequences of doing drugs. Just for the sake of some sort of intoxication, hallucination or pleasure, they would try intoxicants, which would eventually evolve towards their getting addicted and once addicted, it became very difficult to come out of that condition. It affected health, finances, family relations and whatnot. He thought of all

Chapter 31

those energetic young boys and girls in the restaurant that day who were full of enthusiasm. It would all vanish. Rahul had read about half a dozen novels on this subject and by the time he came to the end of each novel, he would feel intense hatred for all those involved in drug trafficking. At the same time, he would detest even more the people who supported these drug mafias: the politicians and bureaucrats. They were supposed to stop such rackets and gangs from operating. Instead, they themselves got involved; the roots were so deep and thick. It was perhaps not possible for a normal citizen to even conceive how deep the tentacles had crept into society. Stories about drugs on TV shows or novels depicted hardly ten per cent of what was actually happening. Even their imagination could not fathom the extent of the rot.

It was evening. He got up and made himself a cup of tea. Green tea was his favourite. He dipped the teabag in hot water and returned to the room, cup in hand. The warmth of the sun had vanished by that time. He slowly finished his tea, relishing each sip.

Suddenly, he was grasped by the urge to find out what happened at the end of the novel, whether the NCB was able to nab the mastermind or not. He opened the book. It had thirty-one chapters in total. He started reading the last chapter. As he was reading, his interest grew, and unknowingly he stiffened and sat upright on the chair and continued reading. The scene narrated in the last chapter seemed familiar. He finished reading Chapter 31, closed his eyes and took a deep breath. He couldn't believe it. He reread the last chapter. He could remember the scenario and it was narrated exactly in the same order. *It was a factual scene.* The last chapter was not fiction but fact. He immediately flipped the pages and read chapters 30 and 29 in the reverse order. The events narrated in these two chapters were fictitious, imagined by the author. That meant that Chapter 1 to

Chapter 30 were a figment of the author's imagination, but the last chapter was not of his creation. He wouldn't even say that it was based on facts because it was a fact in itself.

He saw the preliminary pages. It was explicitly written as usual:

This is a work of fiction. The names, characters and places in the book are the product of the author's imagination, or are used fictitiously. Any resemblance to any person, living or dead, events or locations is entirely coincidental.

He knew that the author's claim wasn't correct as far as the last chapter was concerned. It wasn't a correct disclaimer. His mind was reeling. The event narrated in the last chapter was known by three people, none of whom would divulge. How did the author come into possession of such information? He wondered whether it was the last chapter that had made *The Grass* a bestseller. No, that couldn't be the reason. The public in general was unaware of the happenings as narrated in the final chapter. For them, it would amount to an anticlimax.

For the first time, he saw the copyright page which routinely mentioned relevant information of the author, the publisher and the printer. He saw it was self-published. He, in fact, wasn't aware of the exact meaning of self-publishing. He noted that there wasn't a publisher's name. Instead, the author, Ashutosh's, email address was mentioned.

Rahul's curiosity was piqued. He would have to find out. It was unbelievable. He was in two minds, whether he should contact the author or not. He gave himself some time to think over it. It took him about an hour to weigh the pros and cons and he finally decided to contact the author.

Chapter – 7

For a long time, Ashutosh had nursed a desire. It was to go on a vacation to the Maldives, an archipelago situated in the Indian Ocean. It wasn't far away from India, nor was a visa necessary but every time he checked travel websites, he found the resorts and hotels in Maldives expensive. His wife Sujata had shown him a number of photographs of the beautiful beaches of Maldives that had been uploaded on the net by tourists. The resorts were equally attractive and offered wonderful amenities. In the last couple of months, some money had been transferred to his account as part of the sale proceeds of his book *The Grass*. It was an additional income and they both decided to take a long vacation. They booked a resort on an island in the Maldives for fifteen days.

Unaware of the developments in New Delhi, or that Spellers was desperately trying to trace him, they were enjoying their stay. It was the eleventh day and for them it was a dream come true. They had hired the most expensive villa of the resort that had an independent swimming pool. The beach, of course, was all around; they had to just step out of the villa. It was the cleanest white sand beach they had ever seen. After breakfast at a twenty-four-hour restaurant, they proceeded to an isolated spot on the beach. They were wearing beach clothes. Ashutosh lay down on the sand; Sujata headed towards the ocean for a dip. She was a good swimmer and had always enjoyed the water. After swimming for about fifteen minutes, Sujata shouted to Ashutosh, 'Why don't you come and join me?'

'Are you enjoying yourself?'

'Yeah, but I'll enjoy even more if you join me! We'll swim together.'

Ashutosh, who preferred to stay on the beach, reluctantly got up and joined Sujata. They started splashing water on each other, swam for a while and then embraced each other. It was a wonderful time for the couple. After another half an hour or so in the water, they grew tired, came out and sat in their respective beach chairs.

'The last ten days were like a dream,' said Sujata, looking at Ashutosh contentedly.

'Are you happy?'

'Uh-huh. This has been possible thanks to your novel.'

Ashutosh laughed, 'I never thought it would sell like this.'

'You should be thankful to uncle, Ashutosh.'

'Definitely. I don't know how he managed all this.'

'He made you one of the bestselling authors in the world.'

Ashutosh said, 'In the world?'

'Don't you think uncle has taken an extraordinary interest in marketing your book?'

'Yes, he has,' Ashutosh replied happily.

'But I still can't understand why he had asked you not to get your photograph printed on the back cover.'

'You've said this umpteen number of times, Sujata, and I've told you I simply followed his advice,' despite himself, a hint of exasperation crept into Ashutosh's voice.

A couple walked past them. They waved to them and smiled. Sujata saw the woman was carrying *The Grass*. 'See, your book is famous here too,' she said with pride.

'Yeah, I saw it at the gift shop the other day.'

'Had there been your picture on the book, these people would have recognized you,' Sujata pursued her pet peeve.

Ashutosh sighed. 'Maybe or maybe not. Tell me, how many times have you tried to match a photograph of Ayn Rand or John Grisham with the men or women you see.

Chapter 31

You've read so many books of theirs. If John Grisham is on this island, would you be able to recognize him?'

'No, unless somebody points him out to me,' Sujata gave in laughingly.

'That's why I say, photograph or no photograph, it doesn't matter.'

Sujata stood up and said, 'Let's go back to the hotel. We'll be leaving for Male at 2 p.m. I don't want to miss it; I've been looking forward to seeing the city and doing some shopping.'

'There's still time.'

'Come on, Ashutosh, I'm tired now. We'll rest a bit too.' She leant forward and kissed him passionately.

They trooped back to the hotel. Ashutosh took a shower, after which he decided to take a nap and Sujata joined him.

******

All authors, journalists, professors, scriptwriters, socialists, businesspersons, book distributors and the like were invited to the annual literary festival being held at the convention hall of New Delhi's Ashoka Hotel. There was a book-reading session, a book launch, interviews of authors and some speeches that were made by professors. Once the programme was over, the illustrious gathering started interacting with each other over drinks and dinner.

One of the invitees was Vinay Mehta, the proprietor of Mehta Book Depot. He was the largest importer and distributor of all kinds of books; his office was in Connaught Place's Middle Circle. The import or procurement of books as well as further distribution had been firmly established over a period of time, and he distributed books all over India. He didn't bother with the nitty-gritties anymore and only monitored the details occasionally. His staff was quite experienced. He was hardly aware of the genre of books being sold. His only concern was that the books, irrespective of title or author, should sell and cash flow shouldn't stop. Vinay Mehta had made a tidy amount of money in the past and lived in a palatial house in Lutyens' Delhi, the upscale neighbourhood, famous for the rich and powerful.

Anand and Sheela entered the convention hall and looked around. People of all sizes and shape were conversing and discussing, wine glass in hand. Anand saw Vinay Mehta and Kalyani sitting at a table. They waved to each other and Vinay signalled them to join him. The duo made their way to his table and after the initial greetings, settled down.

'So, how is business?' Anand asked Vinay.

'As usual. How are you doing?' Vinay grinned and continued, 'I'm dependent on Spellers for my bread and butter!' He looked at Sheela, who reciprocated with a smile.

Kalyani was surreptitiously checking out Sheela. Sheela was rich. Sheela was beautiful. Sheela was always stylishly attired. Kalyani had met her on various occasions and every time she found herself secretly admiring her. She was at the same time somewhat jealous of her. Kalyani looked at Anand. He was a carefree dashing personality, though short of money, but Sheela's company compensated that one shortcoming. Drinks were served to them.

Kalyani said, 'Sheela, I heard you're running after an author. Since when has Spellers started doing this?' The tone was mocking.

Anand didn't like it. He said, 'Kalyani, Spellers is always in search of good work. Spellers wants the best of them. One gets a feeling of satisfaction after a win, particularly when the person is the best in his profession.'

Kalyani got embarrassed. Before she could react, Sheela said smoothly, 'Kalyani, you're looking very pretty in that outfit. All the men here would want to talk to you.'

Chapter 31

'And the women too,' Vinay said, as he put his empty wine glass on the table.

Sheela continued in the same smooth silky voice, 'I'd love to run after you, if you start writing the reviews yourself instead of forwarding a pre-written review to your editor.'

This was too much for Kalyani. It was a direct attack. Everybody knew it but no one talked about it, particularly in public.

Trying to save the situation from a possible flare-up, Anand interrupted, 'Kalyani, please, you know why Sheela said what she did. She's trying to reach one particular author.'

'And getting desperate,' Kalyani added, sipping her wine.

'Yes. You see, she only wants your assistance. Shankar had spoken with you.'

'But he wasn't rude. She is–'

'Forget it, Kalyani, let's enjoy each other's company and this wonderful evening,' Anand smiled at her charmingly, and in a barely audible voice addressed Sheela, 'Kalyani may still help you.'

Sheela smiled at him and whispered, 'You're a dear friend.' She got up gracefully and walked over to where Kalyani was seated at the table. She sat down beside her.

Vinay was unconcerned. He was enjoying his drink and the presence of the ladies. He asked, 'Which author are you talking about?'

'There's a book, *The Grass*,' replied Anand.

'Yes, I know, what about it?'

'You know?' The words came out before an astonished Anand could stop himself.

'Yes, yes, I know because I'm importing it, in large quantities.'

'Importing?' Both women questioned in unison.

'Yes, and now you must be surprised, how I know. It's because initially I declined but my supplier in the USA said that I wouldn't have to pay any money. It is on an on-sale basis.'

'What do you mean by on-sale basis?' Kalyani asked him, eyes narrowed.

'This means, my supplier will book the sale only after it's sold at my end. I've to make the remittances only after I get the same from my retailers.'

'That means, he offered you the book free of cost?' Kalyani was incredulous.

'No, not free of cost. In fact, in case of all other suppliers, we're to make the payment to the banker and only after that we can claim delivery from the port. But in the case of this supplier, we were not required to make any payment at the time. The arrangement is that when the books are sold by retailers, only then our liability arises for making payment to the supplier and that too after deducting our commission. Moreover, all shipping charges, insurance, damages, sales return are also his headache. So, the terms were attractive. I only need to keep an inventory. That's all,' Vinay explained.

'That's really smart on his part. He started dumping the books,' Sheela mused.

'Dumping will not be the right word because the book is selling. At this stage, now, if the supplier intends to change the terms, saying that the delivery will be made only on payment, I may have to agree. You see, it is in demand. You yourself are interested in publishing it. Are you not?'

'Yes, I am,' Sheela admitted.

'How many copies have you imported so far?' asked Anand.

'I don't exactly remember but may be around two lakhs.'

'Two lakhs? And all sold?'

'I've distributed almost all except a few, say roughly, ten thousand copies are still lying with me.'

Chapter 31

Kalyani was listening intently to the conversation, and thinking fast. All the investment had been made by someone in the USA and not in India. Then, in probability, the author, though Indian, may have migrated to the USA and Spellers was trying to contact him here in India.

'Sheela, Ashutosh might be living in the US, as the books are coming from there,' Kalyani said.

Sheela shook her head, 'You may be right but there's one fact to consider: he applied for the ISBN here in India and got the first four thousand copies printed here.'

Anand chipped in, 'Yes, you're right. He may be living abroad but one thing is certain – after investing in four thousand copies here, he got an investor in the USA, who is not only getting the book printed but also doing all sorts of promotion and marketing. That requires more money when compared to printing.'

They continued discussing the issue for some more time and then got up to get some food.

******

Ashutosh and Sujata were back from Male. It was 8 p.m. Sujata prepared a cup of tea for herself in the room. Ashutosh wasn't interested in tea and wanted a hard drink. About an hour later, they headed to a Mexican restaurant for dinner. Since the resort catered to different kinds of tourists, it offered a wide range of cuisines. They had an Indian restaurant, a Continental restaurant and one which specialized in Oriental, Arabian and Japanese cuisines. Sujata and Ashutosh had tried different cuisines, but most of the time in the Indian restaurant. That evening, they wanted to try Mexican. In the resort, one had to call the restaurant and reserve a table at least an hour prior to dining. They had booked their table beforehand, and were escorted to it. They sat down.

Sujata said, beaming, 'It's like we are in heaven.'

Ashutosh said gleefully, 'All thanks to *The Grass*.'

'Yeah. This is really a beautiful place, wonderful culinary delights …'

'And amazing drinks.'

He had tried new cocktails of all types, the names of which he had learnt only at that resort. The food, and particularly the drinks, were all expensive. Pretty expensive. Very few people might be aware that no drinks were allowed into the Maldives. The customs wouldn't even allow a bottle of water. If you were carrying one, you'd be asked to dispose of it before you left the airport. The Maldives government wanted to earn more and more revenue from tourists and they charged heavily for drinks. That also added to their revenue.

They ordered some seafood and one plate of vegetable enchiladas.

'What's that?' Sujata asked.

'I don't know. I liked the name and I ordered it,' Ashutosh said nonchalantly.

'What if we don't like it?'

'Don't worry, we'll order something else.'

'You're spending a lot,' Sujata sniffed disapprovingly.

'Yes, but I've made a budget. We still have money for the next four days.'

Exactly at that time, his phone rang. He answered the call and listened attentively. He spoke for about five minutes before hanging up. Sujata looked at him questioningly.

'Uncle called. We'll have to leave tomorrow morning.'

'What? Why?' gasped Sujata, shocked.

'I know you're enjoying this holiday – we're enjoying this long-awaited vacation – but we have to cut short this trip.'

Chapter 31

'But why, Ashutosh?'

'Uncle wants me to meet somebody tomorrow evening in Delhi,' Ashutosh informed Sujata, taking in her crestfallen expression.

'Is it so urgent?' Sujata couldn't hide her disappointment.

'I don't know but it is related to the book.'

'We can delay that. You can meet him after four more days. You should have told uncle,' Sujata tried to reason with him, hoping against hope.

'Sujata, we've already spent eleven days here. I would have asked him if we'd spent only a couple of days here. But now, I couldn't tell him that. Moreover, there was this note of urgency in his voice that I can't overlook.'

'Oh, no,' Sujata said.

'Don't worry, darling, we've enjoyed enough,' he tried to console her. 'This will remain a memorable trip.'

Sujata felt dejected. She had always been certain that uncle had some hidden agenda behind the book, which they were unaware of.

Chapter – 8

Ganesh Salakar had seen the email. It was short.

Dear Ashutosh,

I have read your book 'The Grass'. It is a nice piece of work. I congratulate you. Can we meet at your convenience? I want to discuss the contents of your book.

Feel free to contact at the number given below.

With regards,

Rahul Mehra

Rahul Mehra had given his phone number at the end of the email. Ganesh had seen the earlier emails sent by Spellers. He hadn't considered it necessary to mention those to Ashutosh. This email, though short, had aroused his curiosity and he wondered what this gentleman wanted to discuss. He had immediately spoken with Ashutosh and insisted that the latter contact Rahul at the given phone number and fix up a meeting ASAP. The earliest would only be the next day evening as Ashutosh was in the Maldives. Other than instructing Ashutosh to choose a high-end place as the venue for the meeting, he had also advised Ashutosh to be formal yet friendly and restrict himself to only listening to what this man had to say.

Although they were in no way related, Ganesh Salakar was the man Ashutosh addressed as 'uncle'.

******

Sanjeev, Shankar and Ayesha had assembled in Sheela's cabin the morning after the literary festival at Ashoka Hotel, which Sheela and Anand had attended. Sheela had told the office boy to bring coffee for everyone.

Chapter 31

'There's news,' Sheela announced. 'Last evening at an event I met Vinay – Vinay Mehta of Mehta Book Depot. He said that he was importing *The Grass* from the US.'

'Importing? How can that be? I met the printer here,' Shankar was astounded.

'You were right. It appears that the first four thousand copies were printed here but thereafter someone in the USA is helping the writer by getting the book printed there and he has also taken the responsibility of marketing *The Grass*.'

'It's a mediocre book. I've read it. Why would anyone invest their money on such a venture?' Ayesha was baffled.

'But the person, whosoever he is, has done the job in a professional manner and has been successful in making it one of the top bestsellers,' Sheela pointed out.

They were silent as the office boy entered with the coffee. He placed the cups of coffee on the table and departed, quietly shutting the door behind him.

'He may not have earned much. The investment might have exceeded the revenue from the book,' Shankar commented, as he and the others picked up a cup each.

'Probably,' Sheela agreed.

Sanjeev, who had been listening so far, said, 'But it's not proper to get a book printed from the US and put the address of the printer who is here in India.'

'What is improper? Is there some violation of law? It's the writer's choice to get his book printed wherever he wants – unless the printer here objects to having his name used thus,' Sheela said.

Sanjeev was unable to follow the whole pattern. The whole sequence looked bizarre. He asked Ayesha, 'You've gone through the book. It's not that good. Yet, money is being invested and not for revenue, nor for popularity. There must be some other reason. What could be the reason?'

Sanjeev was right, Sheela thought. However, she cut in before Ayesha could respond, 'Look, Sanjeev, we're not here to investigate the reason. That's not our job. We're in the business of books. We don't have to think beyond that.'

They all kept quiet. Sheela had always had her priorities in order. Now too, she didn't want to divert her focus.

Sheela changed the topic. She asked Sanjeev briskly, 'What happened to Mrs Srinivasan's book?'

'That's for you to decide, ma'am. If you give the green signal, we can go ahead.'

'Her husband called the other day and was again asking about publishing her book.'

'Ma'am, we can go ahead and publish it.'

'Ayesha, you've seen the book. What do you think? How many copies can we sell?'

'I'm not sure. It's meant only for a selective audience,' Ayesha replied.

'Why don't you ask her how many copies she'll buy?' Sheela turned to Sanjeev.

'I'll ask her.'

'Sanjeev, get only that many books printed. Let Mrs Srinivasan buy the whole lot. If there's a demand, we'll print on demand.'

'Okay,' Sanjeev nodded.

As the three trooped out of her cabin, Sheela found her thoughts going back to the *The Grass*. Truth be told, Sheela too was curious to find out the reason behind the novel's popularity. She started checking her emails. She had asked Ayesha to forward the manuscript, which had been sent to Scholars. She glanced through the pages. It was about 270 pages; when formatted, it would roughly come to about 300 pages. She closed the file and checked the other emails.

******

Chapter 31

Ashutosh and Sujata reached home by about 4 p.m.

The time fixed for the meeting was 7 p.m. at the tea lounge of the Taj Hotel. Rahul entered the lobby of the Taj Hotel at 7 p.m. sharp. It was tastefully decorated; there were chairs and sofas in the middle of the lobby. Rahul had never been to this luxurious hotel. He smiled at the girl welcoming him at the entrance, and asked her about the tea lounge. She directed him towards the far end of the lobby, where the tea lounge was located.

Rahul stepped down the three stairs and there was the tea lounge, tables arranged in a semicircle overlooking a small waterfall. He saw a young man, about thirty-five years of age, sitting at a corner table. It had only two chairs, one of which was occupied by him. He got up on seeing Rahul, guessing that he might be the gentleman who had sent the email. Ashutosh came a little forward and enquired, 'Mr Mehra?'

'Yes … Ashutosh?'

'Yes, sir,' Ashutosh smiled. 'Good evening, sir.'

They sat down.

Ashutosh politely gazed at the man in his mid-sixties, sitting in front of him.

'Good evening. You're a young man. I was expecting someone of my age. People usually start writing in mid-age. May I call you Ashutosh?'

'Sure, sir.'

The waiter came with a menu card and requested their order. They both ordered Darjeeling tea. He picked up the menu and went away.

'My congratulations, Ashutosh. Your novel is doing very well. It is among the top ten bestsellers. I saw it at Amsterdam airport on my way back from the US and picked up a copy.'

'Thank you, sir.'

'Is this your profession?' Rahul asked, trying to size Ashutosh up.

'No sir, I'm a lecturer of English literature at Delhi University. It was at the back of my mind for quite some time to write fiction. I had started writing about two years back. I wrote a few chapters. Then I left it for a couple of months. After two months, when I again started writing, I forgot the character I had conceived. I had to go back all over, read again. I placed myself in the story again. And like that, the same situation was repeated once again but ultimately I finished it. It took me about a year. It is my first attempt.'

The tea arrived.

'But it was really a good attempt. Becoming a bestseller at the first attempt itself is, undoubtedly, admirable.'

'It just happened. I hadn't expected it would go this far,' Ashutosh replied modestly.

'Where did you get the idea of picking up the subject? The drugs, the mafia and all that. It's strange because you're a student of literature. They don't teach these subjects in literature. As far as I know, it is Lawrence, Eliot and all these sorts of authors, the classic ones which are there in English literature.'

'That's right, sir. But nobody reads such stuff these days. The public is more interested in crime, thriller and suspense. You look at the list of bestsellers of the last few years. Except Ayn Rand, it is the mystery writers who sell.

I started reading about drugs, for the simple reason that one of my college friends got addicted to drugs. It was pitiable. His parents put him in a rehab centre for six months. He came back healthy and fine, but gradually he turned to it again. He was unstoppable. His health started deteriorating. During his last days, I had gone to meet him,' Ashutosh paused, his eyes had a faraway look, as though he had returned to that moment of his college life.

Chapter 31

He resumed after awhile, 'He was on his bed but he was just a skeleton. I think his weight wouldn't have been more than 25–30kg at that time. He used to be such a healthy, jovial and intelligent fellow. It came as a shock. It took me more than six months to recover from the shock that my friend had passed away. I decided to find out how drugs work on one's body and how, in spite of its ban all over the world, an addict gets it easily anywhere. It's delivered at home, you know.'

'Yes, I know,' Rahul said, quietly. He had listened carefully to the young man in front of him. Whatever Ashutosh had said was the story of every addict. The end result was death. He could see that Ashutosh's eyes had moistened. He asked gently, 'Do you still remember him?'

'Yes, a lot.'

'I'm sorry about him. But one can't do anything beyond a point. Such people write their own fate.'

They finished their tea.

'Sir, you wanted to talk to me about the contents of my book,' Ashutosh reminded him.

Rahul too was ready to get to the reason why he had sought this meeting. He took a deep breath and asked, 'Yes, Ashutosh, the book you've written, *The Grass*, is it all fiction?'

'Yes, sir. All the characters are fictitious. The story is from my imagination. In fact, everything is imaginary. Why do you ask?' Ashutosh looked at Rahul curiously.

'Are you sure? It's all fiction?'

'Definitely.'

'And you wrote it?'

Now that was irritating. He said, 'Yes, sir. I wrote it.'

'Please don't get annoyed. The climax, the last chapter of the book, seems to resemble some actual facts.'

'The last chapter? Chapter 31?'

'Yes.'

'Sir, I had actually finished my book at Chapter 30. My original manuscript had thirty chapters.'

'Then ...?' Rahul prodded.

'Then, I was trying to get it published,' Ashutosh gestured, opening the palm of both hands. 'You know how difficult it is for a first-time author. I discussed with my uncle. He suggested that I forward the manuscript to him. He has an excellent command over the English language. He said he'd read it, edit it and help me with its printing.'

'You were to tell me about Chapter 31.'

'Yes. My uncle finalized the script and he added Chapter 31. When I asked him, he told me that the last chapter was important and that the climax matters. I read the same and of course I approved it and, thereafter, I'd say he almost took over everything about the book. He's instrumental in the success of the book.'

'Who is this uncle?' Rahul asked, intrigued.

'Sir, his name is Ganesh Salakar. He's not really my uncle – he was my professor in college. I was his favourite student,' here Ashutosh smiled slightly, his eyes crinkling. 'Gradually our bond strengthened. I became a lecturer and I started calling him uncle. He retired about two years ago.'

Rahul reflected on all that he had just heard. So Ashutosh didn't know anything. The last chapter wasn't written by him. It was inserted later on. He would have to meet 'uncle'.

'Can I meet him?' he asked abruptly.

'Sir, is there some problem with the last chapter? You're saying it resembles some facts known to you.' Ashutosh hoped he sounded casual.

'I never said "known to me",' corrected Rahul. 'Yes, the situation narrated therein seems familiar.'

'I'll talk to my uncle and let you know.'

'Can you talk to him right now?' Rahul urged him.

Chapter 31

Ashutosh took out his mobile and called Ganesh Salakar. He got up and went to the lobby. He came back after about ten minutes and smiled at Rahul. 'Sir, my uncle will meet you tomorrow at this place itself.'

'Thank you. At what time?'

'At 11.30 a.m. Will that be okay with you, sir? I'm sorry I forgot to ask you about the timings before speaking with him.'

'No problem. I'll be here at the appointed time. Can you please give me his mobile number?'

Ashutosh gave his uncle's number to Rahul, after which they both departed.

Chapter – 9

Rahul was at his home, preparing his dinner and thinking about the meeting earlier that day at the Taj Hotel. He had found Ashutosh to be a genuine person. He appeared to Rahul like one of those members of the teaching profession who were not much aware of the intricacies involved in the fibre of social structure. It seemed like his friend's death from drug addiction had goaded him to pen the book. His uncle had inserted the last chapter and definitely with some agenda. Rahul had also got the impression that Ashutosh had never been told about that hidden purpose. Ashutosh was interested in publishing and marketing the book, a job which was effectively undertaken by his uncle.

His dinner ready, Rahul sat at the table to eat. He switched on CNN, the news channel. Yet another discussion was underway on the presidential election in America, which was to be held in the coming months.

He finished his dinner, cleared the table, switched off the TV, and picked up *The Grass*. He turned to the last chapter.

Chapter 31

It was early morning. The minister was an early riser. He normally gave appointments to his close friends, relatives or people from his constituency for personal meetings between 7 a.m. and 9.30 a.m. At 10 a.m., he would leave for his office. That morning, at 7 a.m. sharp, a man came to meet the minister. The meeting was fixed on priority. The minister and his visitor, a white man, sat down at the table and the staff was asked to serve breakfast.

At 7.30 a.m., there was another visitor, who was the senior officer of the enforcement agency pertaining to drugs and narcotics. He greeted the minister.

'Jai Hind.'

Chapter 31

'Jai Hind. Come, have a seat.'

The officer sat down. The usual greetings were exchanged. The minister confirmed, 'Are you the chief of the NCB?'

'Yes, sir.'

'What's your name?'

'Umesh Kumar, sir.'

'Oh yes, my PA told me. How long have you been posted here?'

'Sir, for about six months.'

'How is it going?'

'What, sir? NCB?'

'Yes, of course. I'm talking to you about your organization.' *There was a touch of arrogance.*

The cook came in and placed some toasts, an omelette, and bread rolls stuffed with mashed potatoes on the table. After a few minutes, the cook returned and placed steamed idlis, freshly prepared.

The minister asked the white man, 'What would you like to have?'

The man looked at all the dishes, smiled and picked up a toast and the omelette and in a very well-mannered way thanked the minister. The minister asked Umesh Kumar to help himself. Umesh Kumar picked up the idlis and a bread roll. After awhile, all three started eating. All of a sudden, the minister said to Umesh Kumar, 'What is the update on the case prepared yesterday?'

Umesh Kumar was expecting the same because he had been called by the minister for briefing.

'Sir, our officers have been gathering information on a drug syndicate. They were keeping surveillance for the last three months. They got a tip that yesterday a delivery of a specific drug would be made at a place in old Delhi. They reached the spot an hour prior to the time the drug was reported to be delivered. They kept watch. At the fixed time, two men came in a van. They were carrying two suitcases. They went inside the house, which was being watched. After five minutes, our officers went inside. Three men were already there. In total, five men were there. One of them took out a gun and pointed it at our officers. As a matter of chance, two of our officers were also carrying their respective guns. They responded immediately and targeted all five.'

'Did any firing take place?'

'No, sir. They wanted to scare our officers because they weren't expecting our officers to carry guns. They surrendered. Sir, it otherwise requires guts to hit government officers on duty. Search was conducted and 30kg of heroin in two suitcases was found. This was meant to be delivered there. We brought all the five men to our office for interrogation and the heroin has been detained.'

'Did your officers find some sort of record there?'

Umesh Kumar was surprised because the records were not discussed anywhere. How did the minister know?

'Well, what about the records?' The minister asked again.

'Two laptops were recovered from the car. These have been detained.'

'What information do the laptops contain?'

'These are in the process of being opened. The officers have to check the laptops. These are locked. The officers are trying to find the password so that they can access the files. Prima facie it appears that these may contain the details of the network in India or may be part of some syndicate.'

The cook, who had been standing in a corner, came in with pots of tea and coffee. He poured tea for Umesh Kumar and the minister. The white man wanted coffee. The dishes were removed.

The minister said, 'Your officers have done a good job. Do they normally act like this?'

'Yes, sir.'

Chapter 31

Umesh Kumar was feeling uncomfortable. He wasn't happy giving such details to the minister in the presence of a third person. He kept looking at him off and on. But the white man was perhaps not interested in their conversation. The minister could also feel Umesh Kumar's discomfort but that wasn't his concern. He continued.

'Are NCB officers allowed to carry guns?'

'Sir, these are licensed guns issued to them officially.'

'Oh, I see. And they always carry it?'

'Not necessarily. Maybe they thought that guns would be needed considering the location of the house.'

'What location?'

'Sir, it was at the dead end of a narrow by-lane in old Delhi.'

'Okay. Do you have anything more to add?'

'No, sir, there's no more to say as of now.'

'Will you wait in the room outside? I have some business to finish.'

Umesh Kumar stood up and went to a waiting room. He felt relieved. He had been called by politicians a number of times during his service tenure. They had their own compulsions. He sat down on a sofa and looked around. A simple room, moderately furnished.

After about fifteen minutes, the minister called him back. He said to Umesh Kumar, 'Now, listen carefully. This is between you and me. It is to be taken seriously.'

'Yes, sir.'

'Release all five men and release the drugs, which had been detained.'

Umesh Kumar stood still. He couldn't believe what he heard. Never before had he been given such instructions. He said, 'Sir ...'

The minister said sternly this time, 'Release means release. No ifs and buts.'

'Sir, kindly listen.'

'Don't tell me that you want these orders in writing. Such things are never given in writing.'

'I know, sir. It is not between you and me. The officers who have risked their life in performing their duty will get demoralized. What do I tell them?'

'Who is the chief? You or them? It is for you to find out the way, you have to convince them,' snapped the minister.

'In a drug's case it isn't possible, sir.'

'You are being insubordinate!'

'It is not like that, sir, but releasing the drugs isn't possible. The news has spread far and wide. The other officers in NCB also know about it. It isn't possible to release it.'

The minister kept quiet. He looked at the white man. They glanced at each other. After thinking for awhile, the minister instructed, 'Okay, don't release the drugs. Make it an unclaimed seizure.'

'Unclaimed?'

'Yes,' the minister said grimly.

'Okay, sir.'

'And release all the five men and give back the laptops,' the minister said and stood up. Umesh Kumar was about to say something when the minister warned him once again, 'No more arguments.'

'Sir, during the interrogation, the men have revealed that the whole network is an international syndicate headed by one Paul.'

'I know,' the minister said.

'You know?' Umesh Kumar said, bewildered.

'Mr Paul is here.' The minister smiled and gestured at the white man who had been sitting there throughout the meeting.

It came as a shock to Umesh Kumar. He had no courage to further counter him.

Chapter 31

The drugs were seized, the five men were released and the laptops were returned.

That was the end of Chapter 31. That was the end of *The Grass*. That was the climax. Rahul wondered whether this particular chapter was intentionally inserted to make *The Grass* the bestseller or it became the bestseller because of Chapter 31.

Chapter – 10

As Ashutosh and Sujata finished their dinner, Sujata asked, 'So, according to Mr Mehra, the contents of the last chapter of your book are similar to some facts?'

'Yes, according to him,' Ashutosh replied as he picked up their dishes and placed them in the kitchen sink.

'And he wanted to talk to you just to tell you this?' Sujata asked, as she mopped the table clean.

'He told me that much,' Ashutosh nodded, putting the leftovers into the fridge. 'Maybe he would have spoken more about it but when I told him that I'd written the first thirty chapters and the last chapter was inserted by my uncle, he didn't talk further.'

'Why?'

'I don't know but he said he'd like to meet uncle and I fixed up their meeting for tomorrow.'

Sujata thought about it. Though she had read the book, she wasn't aware of the contents of Chapter 31. In fact, she had read it at the manuscript stage, when Ashutosh was trying to get it published. She picked up the book and opened Chapter 31. She read it. She was hoping to reread something. But she hadn't been told that the new chapter had been inserted by uncle. Ashutosh had simply told her that uncle had carried out some changes in the manuscript and that it was a 'sort' of editing. It took her not more than fifteen minutes to finish the chapter. It was a short chapter.

'Ashutosh, did Mr Mehra say it's a fact, or, to put it better, it resembles some factual situation?' she asked again.

'That's right,' Ashutosh stifled a yawn.

'There are three characters in this chapter: a minister, Mr Paul and Umesh Kumar. That means, one of these three

Chapter 31

men had narrated the incident to uncle or to someone else, who in turn informed uncle,' Sujata's eyes widened as she expressed her thoughts aloud to Ashutosh.

'May be … possible. Uncle might have thought that inserting such an incident in the last chapter would make the book more interesting.'

'But he could have altered facts, so that it wouldn't offend anyone or be a cause of embarrassment.'

'I'll talk to uncle about this,' Ashutosh assured her, getting ready to go to bed.

'That's okay. But what's more interesting is how Mr Mehra knows that the incident narrated in the book is an actual incident.' Sujata was all worked up now, pacing up and down in their bedroom.

'Somebody might've told him.'

'No,' she shook her head. 'If that had been the case, he wouldn't have been so interested. No one would take the pain to meet the author unless it relates to him personally.'

Ashutosh mulled over it and said slowly, 'You're right; Mr Mehra first showed interest in meeting me and then wanted to meet uncle.'

'He would be eager to find out how the facts narrated in the chapter reached uncle.'

'Definitely.'

'We should talk to uncle about this.'

'Yes, I'll talk to him.'

'What I mean is that before uncle meets Mr Mehra, we should talk to uncle; we should be aware of the facts before they talk.'

'How does it matter, Sujata?' Ashutosh was getting impatient now. He'd had a tiring day and all this talk about Mr Mehra, uncle and *The Grass* was getting under his skin now.

'It matters, Ashutosh. You're the author. You have some responsibility. You're answerable. If Mr Mehra intends to take some sort of legal action, it would be against you and not uncle,' Sujata got into bed, feeling annoyed with Ashutosh for not being able to grasp the consequence of this new and unexpected revelation.

'Sujata, you're unnecessarily worrying. I'm sure uncle will handle him. Moreover, they're meeting tomorrow morning at 11.30. We can't meet uncle before that. We don't have time in the morning. Let them meet, we'll go and see uncle tomorrow evening.'

Sujata shrugged. But she was a little worried. Despite his nonchalant stance, Ashutosh too was thinking about the implications.

******

At 11.30 a.m. sharp, Rahul entered the lobby. He now knew where the tea lounge was located, and strode towards it. Once there, he looked around but couldn't see anyone who he could guess was waiting for him. He sat down.

Ganesh Salakar was sitting in the lobby and saw him entering the reception area. He saw him walking towards the tea lounge purposefully. Ganesh had never seen Rahul Mehra but it wasn't difficult to understand that the person he had come to meet had arrived. He kept sitting there. He could see Rahul sitting in the tea lounge. He saw him smile at the waiter who approached him. Perhaps Rahul was telling him that he was expecting someone any time now. Ganesh looked at Rahul's face. It was a hard face, like that of a policeman. Rahul Mehra appeared to be a couple of years older to Ganesh.

After sizing him up for about ten minutes, Ganesh decided it was time he joined Rahul at the tea lounge. He got up and walked towards Rahul. 'Mr Mehra?' he confirmed.

'Yes.'

'I'm Ganesh Salakar.'

Chapter 31

'Please be seated,' Rahul said formally.

Ganesh sat down. Rahul looked at him. A man with a serene face. A well-dressed man with a good accent. Rahul ordered tea for them both, which was served within a few minutes.

Ganesh Salakar said, 'Ashutosh told me you wanted to meet me.'

'That's right. He must have told you the reason.'

'No, not exactly.'

'Okay. He told me you had edited his manuscript and helped in marketing his book.'

'Yes. Both were my students. Bright students,' Ganesh smiled.

'Both?' Rahul raised an enquiring eyebrow.

'Ashutosh and Sujata. They married afterwards. Ashutosh wrote the book. He tried to get it published but as you know, no one was interested in publishing it. So, I helped him. Anyway, please tell me the purpose of this meeting.'

Rahul Mehra looked at him directly. He too wasn't interested in stray talks. He said, 'I'm told you inserted Chapter 31, the final chapter in the novel.'

Ganesh replied, 'Yes, Ashutosh had written thirty chapters. The story ended when the culprits were arrested. I added one more chapter, where it was stated that the culprits were released at the behest of a politician. It was a sort of anticlimax.'

Rahul Mehra wasn't listening. He said bluntly, 'But Chapter 31 is not fiction. It resembles facts. Or to put it another way, it isn't an imaginary creation, as has been claimed at the beginning of the book.'

'Is it so?'

'Yes.'

'Sir, the whole novel is a work of imagination, including the last chapter. What makes you say that it isn't fiction?' Ganesh politely challenged Rahul.

Rahul noted the casualness with which Ganesh was speaking. Was it genuine or was it fake? He said quietly, 'Mr Salakar, the situation in the last chapter is real. It isn't fiction. From where did you get this information?'

'I don't understand, Mr Mehra, why are you insisting on the same thing again and again. The situation is nothing abnormal. I've seen in a number of books and movies that there is a nexus between criminals and politicians. That's nothing new. I got the idea and drafted the last chapter.'

'No, I'm not ready to take all that rubbish.'

Ganesh Salakar's expression changed as he grew serious. He picked up his cup of Darjeeling tea, took a sip and said, 'Okay, let's assume for a moment you're right. There may be certain facts known to you, which you found similar to those given in the last chapter. How does it matter? How does it affect *you*?'

This was something Rahul hadn't expected. He was speechless. He didn't know how to respond. Ganesh was right when he said that it shouldn't affect Rahul. How does one answer that?

Rahul finally asked, 'Who are you?'

Ganesh laughed unpleasantly and countered, 'Who are *you*? You showed interest in meeting me. I never showed interest. I had consented to meet you. *You* have to tell me who *you* are. If you don't want to talk, let's end this meeting. I repeat, the contents in Chapter 31 aren't real. It's purely fictitious.'

'Do you really want to end this meeting right now?' asked Rahul. He could feel anger rising in him.

'Yes, of course. I've come on your request.'

'But I'm sure you have no intention of ending this meeting *right now*.'

Chapter 31

'What makes you so sure?' Ganesh taunted.

'Okay, let's end this,' said Rahul, looking around for a waiter as if he was eager to settle the bill. He smiled at Ganesh and continued, 'You're right that I showed interest in meeting you but from now onwards I know you'll be interested in meeting me.'

Ganesh was intelligent enough to get him. He said slowly, 'You're right. It was I who wanted to meet you.'

'Chapter 31 was intentionally inserted and the marketing of the novel was manipulated to trace me. Am I right?'

'Yes.'

'Who're you?'

'Ganesh Salakar.'

'Nonsense. I know that. I was told you were a professor of English in Delhi University. What are you doing now? For whom are you working?'

'What makes you think I'm working for someone?'

'I'm sure of that. I don't want to talk in circles, Mr Salakar! You have to be straightforward,' suggested Rahul severely.

'Yes, I will but before that you've got to tell me who you are!' Ganesh countered.

'You know that. At least, you must have known by now.'

'I want you to say it.'

'Why? Are you recording this conversation?' bristled Rahul.

'Does it look like that?'

'No,' Rahul admitted.

Ganesh was quiet for some time. All of sudden he said, 'Can we have a second meeting?'

'What's that now?' Rahul demanded.

'Nothing. If you don't want to meet again, I can continue talking.'

'Do you need directions from someone to proceed further?'

'Not exactly,' Ganesh shook his head. 'I'd like someone to meet you.'

'But you too will be there?'

'Yes.'

'Great. When?'

'Maybe today itself. I'll confirm. Is this okay with you?'

'Yes, sure.'

Rahul paid the bill and they came out. At the exit, Rahul said, 'Next time, don't waste your time sitting in the lobby and staring at me.'

Rahul smiled, slightly nodded and approached the valet parking desk to give the attendant the valet parking ticket.

Chapter – 11

It was 1 p.m. Rahul was driving back to his house after his meeting with Ganesh Salakar. He was unaware that his car was being followed. Two people in a white SUV had been waiting just outside the Taj Hotel. They had spotted him when he drove out of the hotel. They had instructions to follow him, simply to find out his address.

The drive to his home from the hotel was about forty-five minutes. As he was coming down the Ridge, he noticed a white SUV in the rear-view mirror. He suddenly realized that he had seen the same vehicle at the last traffic signal, when he had stopped as the light had turned red. He adjusted the mirror and saw the vehicle number. It wasn't difficult to remember the four digits 3345 because these were the last four numbers of his mobile number. He continued driving. He wasn't sure whether he was being followed or not. He thought of verifying the same. It was a vague thought. Why not try it? His home was now only three lanes away and he was to go straight. Instead, he turned right and then entered a lane on the left, which hardly had any traffic at that time. Yes, the white SUV was still there. He continued driving and was quite close to his home. He wanted to park it at a predesignated place, but the white SUV was still behind him. He was sure now. He didn't stop and jumped the red light, turned into a narrow lane on the left and stopped. After a few seconds, he saw the white SUV going straight; clearly, the driver in the white SUV had missed his car – now sitting in the small lane – hoping that he, Rahul, had gone straight.

Rahul returned home.

******

Another meeting was fixed for the same day at 6 p.m., somewhere in Connaught Place. Ganesh Salakar had informed Rahul Mehra. When Ganesh reached home it was around 3 p.m. Ashutosh and Sujata too arrived at Ganesh's house more or less at the same time. Once they were inside and had sat down in the living room, Ashutosh turned to Ganesh.

'Did you meet Mr Mehra?'

'Yes, I met him,' Ganesh confirmed.

'What did he say? Why was he interested in meeting you?'

'I think he spoke to you about the last chapter of your book. He said the same thing to me. According to him, the events of that chapter aren't fictitious but are similar in nature to some facts, which he knows.'

'Did he tell you?'

'No. I told him that it was a work of fiction and that if there is any resemblance, it is a matter of pure coincidence.'

Sujata had been listening intently. She now interrupted, 'Uncle, who is he? Why did he contact first Ashutosh, and then you? There must be a reason behind it.'

Ganesh looked at her and said, 'Yes, I tried to find out who he was and why he was showing so much interest. He evaded answering my questions.'

'Uncle, please tell us honestly. We're worried. Is the narration in the last chapter related to some actual incident? You inserted it in the book. If you say it has been written by you, it's okay. But if not, then who is responsible for it?'

Ganesh looked at her and sighed to himself. He realized he would have to answer Sujata's question. It was a valid question; her concern was not unfounded. Why had anyone come out of the blue and started questioning the unfolding of the events of Chapter 31? Both Ashutosh and Sujata had the right to know.

Chapter 31

He smiled at Sujata and requested, 'Can you please make some tea for all of us?'

'Of course, Uncle, but you haven't answered,' she pointed out, also smiling.

'I'll tell you everything. Please make us some tea.'

Sujata headed to the kitchen and returned to the living room, a few minutes later, carrying a tray with three cups of tea on it. She set it down on the centre table, and sat down.

Ganesh picked up a cup and said, 'Please have tea and relax. I'll tell you how it all happened.'

Both of them picked up their cup, and listened to Ganesh attentively as he spoke.

'When I retired about two years back, I was offered a job at the American library located on Curzon Road. There are about twenty people working there. Six out of those twenty are American citizens; the rest are Indians. I'm one of them. When you gave me your manuscript to go through, on some days, I would carry it with me to the library because there isn't much work every day. When there isn't much work, they don't mind if I do any sort of reading. It so happened that one evening, I'd left the manuscript on my desk. The next day, when I went for work, one of my colleagues, Olivia, an American, approached me. She told me she had glanced through the manuscript and suggested that I end the novel in a different way. I just laughed it away. In the evening, she came up with this chapter and said that I can end the novel with it. I read it and liked it. At that time, I had no idea that it might relate to a true incident. After some slight changes, I added that chapter in your book, Ashutosh.'

Sujata asked, 'But is it related to a real event?'

'Yes,' Ganesh nodded, looking at her. 'I came to know about this at a later stage. Ashutosh, do you remember you had got the first two thousand copies printed here, in Delhi?'

'Yes.'

'At that point of time, Olivia again spoke to me about the book. For the first time, she told me that the narration in the new chapter, which she had handed over to me, was taken from an actual incident. She told me that a racket of drug mafia based in America was busted by the NCB in India but all the suspects were released at the behest of an Indian politician – the NCB chief was instructed by the politician to do so. That American drug mafia king had friends all over the world, who were powerful. The American police had been after him but they weren't able to lay their hand on any evidence against him. He was detained and questioned once but due to lack of evidence, they couldn't arrest him.'

Ganesh stopped to gather his thoughts. He looked at the young couple; both Ashutosh and Sujata were listening quietly.

Ganesh continued, 'She told me that the American police were on the lookout for the NCB chief, who disappeared thereafter and was perhaps retired. They had no intelligence on where he was living after his retirement. The American police had a strong belief that this ex-chief of NCB would definitely be able to tell them a lot about the activities of the drug lord. So, she suggested that they were ready to invest money and popularize *The Grass* all over the world, hoping that someday he might read it and relate it with himself.'

There was a long period of silence as the husband-wife duo digested this revelation. Sujata was the first to speak. She observed in a cold voice, 'So, Ashutosh was misused.'

'No. In fact, I was misused. Ashutosh trusted me and never questioned the authenticity of Chapter 31. I was misused. And I couldn't tell him the background when I came to know the truth because I was told to keep it to myself. If the information got out, the drug mafia could have posed a danger to you. I preferred to remain quiet.'

'Why are you telling us now?' Ashutosh asked, perturbed.

Chapter 31

'Because it appears the ex-chief has been finally traced. That chapter has served its purpose,' Ganesh sounded tired.

Ashutosh was not happy. It was a very unpleasant situation. He had a lot of respect for Ganesh Salakar, who had been a father figure. Sujata had been questioning him all along regarding his uncle taking so much interest in promoting and marketing his book. Ashutosh had a sort of blind faith in his uncle but after listening to the entire story, he was feeling dejected. Ganesh could see the frustration and sadness on his face. He was about to speak, when Sujata spoke.

'Uncle, is Mr Mehra the ex-chief?'

'It looks like that. When I spoke with him this morning, he didn't admit anything but if you carefully note his questions, observations, behaviour and attitude, he's the ex-chief. Olivia is going to meet him in the evening.'

'Uncle, I still can't believe all that you have said just now. Why would the American police go to such lengths to nab a drug smuggler? It doesn't make sense. The methodology used seems rather unusual.'

Ganesh realized that Sujata was raising relevant issues one after the other. He ignored her and addressed Ashutosh instead.

'Ashutosh, look ... what I did was on a bona fide belief that the new chapter was also fictitious. Later, when I came to know the truth, I didn't want to create problems for you and Sujata. The book was becoming popular and they were able to push it to that level. I was happy ... you were happy.'

'But, Uncle, at least you could have told us in confidence.'

'Yes, I should have, but surely you can understand the situation I was in ... how I was trapped into all this.'

'Why did you meet Mr Mehra in the morning? You could have asked Olivia to go and meet him.'

'This is exactly what I had told Olivia but she wanted only me to be there in the first meeting to ensure that he was the person we were looking for.'

Sujata was quick to note the word 'we' iin the last few words spoken by Ganesh. She asked, 'We?'

'Oh,' Ganesh looked a trifle flustered now. 'I'm sorry. I used the first person by mistake. They were looking for him.'

Worried and disappointed, they both got up and without exchanging formalities, silently left Ganesh's home.

******

Seeing them leave distraught and anxious, Ganesh was guilt-ridden. When he joined this new job two years ago, he was told that besides routine work at the library, he might be assigned work which could be different from his profile. Such assignments would be once in a while. He was assured that the work assigned would never be illegal, criminal or in violation of the law of the land. That was one of the terms of the employment contract. When Olivia first asked him to insert the chapter, he wasn't aware that it was one such assignment. He was categorically informed about this being a part of his job description only when Olivia told him that the American police were interested in popularizing the book. He had been told there was nothing illegal about it.

The email address in *The Grass* was his. When Spellers had emailed him expressing their interest in publishing this book under their banner, Olivia had told Ganesh that he needn't reply. However, when he received Rahul's email, Olivia instructed him to respond by sending Ashutosh to meet him. For the next rendezvous with Rahul, he was uninterested in meeting the latter but here too Olivia insisted that he had to go because Ashutosh had referred his name, which was a fact. She had briefed him how much to talk and to judge whether Rahul was the right person they were looking for.

Chapter 31

After the meeting, Ganesh had brought Olivia up-to-date on their discussion. He also told her that Mr Rahul Mehra was particular that the conversation had to be straightforward. He had also suggested the possibility that Rahul might not be available for another meeting and that he had suspected that Ganesh Salakar was only a front man.

******

Justin Brown was a special agent of American intelligence, who was working at the American Center, in New Delhi, and it wasn't uncommon to post intelligence persons to other countries. He was tall, clean-shaven and wore his hair long. Olivia gave Justin details of both the meetings and advised that he should go for the next meeting. She further told Justin categorically that Rahul might refuse any more meetings.

Justin thought over it. He was certain that if Rahul was the man they were looking for, he wouldn't buy all that Olivia had just told him. Moreover, Rahul would not only have to be told why they were looking for him but he would have to be on board if they expected his cooperation. Justin decided to meet him at 6 p.m. that day itself.

Chapter – 12

It was a small, nondescript coffee shop at the Inner Circle of Connaught Place. Rahul had told Ganesh to meet him there and he himself was there exactly at 6 p.m. There must have been sixteen tables, most of which were unoccupied. He selected a corner table and ordered a cappuccino. After five minutes, Justin Brown entered the coffee shop. He saw an elderly person sitting at a corner. Justin walked towards him; Rahul was expecting someone would accompany Ganesh Salakar but Ganesh was not anywhere to be seen.

'Mr Mehra?' Justin enquired softly when he was within earshot.

'Yes.'

'I'm Justin Brown. You can call me Justin,' he smiled politely, as he extended his hand.

'But I was expecting Ganesh Salakar too,' Rahul said as he stood up and shook hands with Justin. He gestured at the other chair for Justin to be seated.

'I preferred to come alone,' Justin said as he sat down.

'Okay. First, I met Ashutosh, then Ganesh Salakar and now you. Is there anyone else?'

Justin laughed and said, 'No, I cut down the third layer.'

'Please introduce yourself.'

As the waiter approached their table on Rahul's signal, Justin paused. Rahul asked him to bring another cup of coffee for Justin, after checking with the American.

'I told you. I'm Justin Brown,' the American responded once the waiter had left.

Rahul grinned, 'Is that sufficient?'

Chapter 31

Justin was about to reply when the waiter served them their coffee. When they both settled down with their coffee, Justin addressed Rahul with a smile.

'No. I'll ask a simple question and then we can take it up from there?'

'Yes?'

'You, Rahul Mehra, resemble the Umesh Kumar in Chapter 31 of *The Grass* because that is a fictional name. Paul, however, is a real name. Is that right?'

Rahul nodded.

'That's great; now we can proceed. You'll appreciate that the confirmation was necessary and it had to be confirmed by you and you alone.'

'What is all this? Why did you arrange all this through a book?' Rahul was intrigued, wondering which way the conversation was headed. 'It was a novel idea, though, I must say.'

'Let me start at the beginning. I'll not hide anything. I request you to listen carefully because everything I say is significant.'

'Sure.'

'Mr Paul Johnson is contesting for the presidential post in our country. He is the nominee of the Republican Party. The other candidate is Sarah Baker, a Democrat. They are the main contenders and the campaign is currently underway. Paul Johnson is a very rich man. He is popular among businesspeople and we have information that his campaign is also being funded from sources outside the USA.'

Justin stopped abruptly and looked at Rahul. He suddenly asked, 'Do you know Paul Johnson?'

Rahul said, 'Please carry on.'

Justin said, 'The wave at present is in favour of Paul Johnson. His campaigning is vigorous. He has hired the best PRs. He has bought the media.'

'So, what? Every politician does that. He's there to win. What's wrong with that?'

'Do I need to tell you what is wrong?' Despite himself, Justin asked him tersely.

'Mr Brown, you haven't introduced yourself till now.'

'I'm sorry, I'm a special agent deputed by the American intelligence agency, the CIA. In fact, the chief of the CIA doesn't approve of Paul Johnson becoming the next president.

Paul Johnson has a shady past. He used to be a drug lord and had a strong network throughout the world. He had powerful friends in almost all countries and he ran his drug business under multiple facades. He made billions and diverted that money to hotels and retail chains.

The country's police, the FBI and intelligence agencies have tried to trap him on many occasions but he couldn't be nabbed because of lack of evidence. He outsmarted them all. About four years back, when he decided to join politics, he buried his past. He came out of the drug business. And now look, he's contesting the presidential election and the way things are going, he may become the next president. Imagine, a drug mafia king becoming the president of the USA. No, our chief will never approve that.'

Justin paused to take a breath and looked at Rahul, who was listening attentively, calmly and patiently.

Justin continued, 'Our chief got the information that on one occasion, he might have left the trial. About ten years back, his network in India was busted. Five men were arrested but they were released the next day. It was you, who released them.'

Rahul preferred to remain silent. He wanted Justin to furnish all details. He said to Justin, 'You may please continue.'

'I was asked to come to India and track you so that if there is a possibility of the existence of any evidence, the

Chapter 31

same could be systematically made public and his campaign could be dented. That's the only weapon we have to reverse the public wave. That's all. I'm sitting here with you,' Justin ended with a slight smile although the expression in his eyes was serious.

'It's not all. I've a few questions.'

'Yes?'

'How did you come to know of the meeting with the minister and how did you manage the actual recreation? Well, almost actual.'

Justin looked at him and smiled. He said, 'We had vague information that Paul's network was once busted in India about ten years back. My chief deputed me to be here. It wasn't possible to contact the minister. Our intelligence had indicated that Paul had met at the minister's residence. We weren't aware of your existence, your involvement. I started looking for a lead. Our local contacts were able to trace the man who worked as a cook at the minister's residence and were able to establish contact with him. Initially, he was reluctant. But money can do miracles.' Here, Justin smiled slightly, tilting his head and looking at Rahul through narrowed eyes.

'He remembered that a senior government officer was called at the minister's residence and was asked to release the detained people. We showed him a photograph of Paul Johnson; he identified him. We asked him to recreate the whole scene. He even remembered exactly what was served.

'We asked him to give an elaborate description. He had overheard most of the conversation. He remembered you being sent to the outer room and when you were called, you were asked to release the arrested men and the drugs. You were reluctant. Then you were asked to only release the men and make the seizure of the drugs as unclaimed. This whole episode was written and when Olivia showed me the manuscript of *The Grass*, the timing was appropriate.'

'Who is Olivia?'

'She's my colleague. She works at the American library here. Ganesh Salakar works with her.'

'So that's how the chapter was inserted,' mused Rahul.

'Yes. We weren't very hopeful of ever being able to reach you. But it was worth taking a chance. Money wasn't a problem. We hired a competent marketing professional in the US and told him that the book should reach every corner of the world. Do you know why?'

'Why?'

'You weren't traceable. We were told that you disappeared immediately after that episode. Your whereabouts weren't known. Nobody knew whether you had left the job and where you had settled, whether in India or in some other country. So, with very little hope, we worked on the book.'

'It was easy.'

'No,' Justin replied immediately, looking stern. 'It wasn't easy. In such a big world, we weren't sure if you had changed your name or citizenship.'

'Okay,' Rahul said after a brief pause. It seemed he had made up his mind to move further in this case. 'I'm here. Tell me what you want from me. I believe everything you have said.'

'Thank you, Mr Mehra. Our chief wants to know if you are in possession of any evidence against Paul Johnson?'

'It was long back. Ten years have passed, Mr Brown. Five men were detained. Heroin was seized. But the men were released. What evidence can there be?'

'You or your staff might have questioned those detained men. Some statements must have been recorded. Some documents must have been prepared.'

'Mr Brown, I think you're presuming too much. How can you presume that I'll tell you anything? Why should I?'

'Mr Mehra, please, I know you cannot be compelled. It's your choice. And never think I'm going to buy you.'

Chapter 31

Rahul smiled. He had the reputation of being the most honest officer of his time.

Justin continued, 'Sir, I can give you a dozen reasons. I can justify the concern of our chief.'

'No need. I agree with his concern. But I've nothing to tell you. If they tell you exactly what happened that day, it would simply be my statement against Paul's. You can manage such statements from anyone. It isn't going to change public perception.'

Justin looked at Rahul and slowly said, 'We were told two laptops were recovered at the time.'

Stiffening, Rahul asked, 'Did the cook tell you that?'

'Yes.'

'Did he not tell you that those were also ordered to be returned?'

'But you or your staff might have opened it,' Justin said hopefully. 'There was one full day in between.'

Rahul realized they had worked hard. They had tried to collect every minute detail.

'No. We couldn't get the password,' Rahul dashed the American's hopes.

'You must have tried?' Justin persisted, despite the creeping hopelessness in his voice.

'My staff had interrogated the detained men. Before my staff could extract something, they were ordered to be released.'

Justin slammed his fist into the palm of his other hand in frustration. Then controlling himself, asked, 'Wasn't there any document?'

'None. Who knew that after ten years the same Paul Johnson would contest the presidential elections in the USA?' Rahul laughed.

Justin's face expressed grave disappointment. His efforts to track Rahul Mehra had yielded nothing.

'Sir ... Mr Mehra ... please recollect something because our chief was hopeful that we'll get some evidence from you. We assure you all protection and confidentiality.'

Rahul grinned and said, 'Tell your chief I wasn't of any help and also tell him not to send people to follow me.'

Justin was taken aback. He admitted apologetically, 'That was my mistake. I overdid it. I didn't want to lose you after so much trouble in tracing you. I'm sorry for that. I just wanted your home address.'

'You could have asked me. When I can come for three meetings, I wouldn't have hesitated to give my address.'

'I'm sorry, sir.'

'Please don't make foolish and rash decisions. Never annoy a person from whom you expect some sort of favour.'

'I'll remember.'

Two hours had passed. They got up.

'Sir, can I expect to have another meeting?' Justin asked.

'I don't think you need another meeting.'

'My chief may need some more feedback.'

'You have my contact number.'

PART – II

Chapter – 13

Sheela Nair got herself cleared from security check and entered the airport lobby holding her business class boarding pass. She was going to Hyderabad, where she was invited to deliver a lecture at the Mass Communication Institute. She hated such lectures as much as she hated reading books but both were essential for a successful professional. She would be returning to Delhi the same evening. There were eateries, souvenir shops, bookshops, etc. She wandered around, waiting for the boarding to be announced. She walked past a bookshop and saw a man taking out *The Grass* from the shelf and glancing at the back cover. His back was towards her but she recognized him. It was Aneesh, her husband. Almost a year had passed since they had last met. She went up to him and touched his shoulder.

Aneesh turned and saw Sheela standing there. He said, 'Oh. What a surprise?'

'How are you, Aneesh?'

'How do I look?' he smiled, turning around to face her fully, straightening up to his full height instinctively.

'Where is the Government of India going?' she asked him teasingly.

Aneesh laughed and said, 'Hyderabad.'

'Me too,' she said, a pleasant expression on her face.

'How is your business doing?' he asked, placing *The Grass* casually back on the shelf.

'As usual,' Sheela replied as she fell in step with him.

'Earning a lot?'

'Business means earning.'

'You're right. Look at us, poor government servants.'

Chapter 31

'Poor?' she said sarcastically.

Aneesh looked at her. She was still very beautiful. She had money to spend on herself. She had inherited the business from her father and was going strong.

'Hey, what are you looking at?' Sheela felt awkward under his intense gaze.

'You see, sometimes I feel it was a mistake to live separately.'

She blushed and said, 'Don't talk nonsense. We've already discussed this several times. Are you going to stay in Hyderabad?'

'No. A Russian cultural delegation is visiting Hyderabad. I'm attending that. I hope to be back tonight or maybe tomorrow morning. What about you?'

'Returning by evening flight.'

'Good.'

Boarding was announced. They said their bye-byes to each other and headed towards the boarding gate.

He was sitting at seat 1B and Sheela was sitting at seat 3C. He was right in front of her. Sheela found herself constantly looking at Aneesh. He was talking to the air hostess. He was a well-mannered man. He had an air of authority about him, yet he was humble. And, he was intelligent. In fact, extra intelligent. He had passed his civil service examination with flying colours and he was given the ministry of his choice. He was working in external affairs and whosoever was the minister, Aneesh was a favourite.

Sometimes, Sheela would wonder why they had separated. He had all the qualities that a woman looks for in a husband. But was it a different cultural background or was it a different lifestyle? Sheela had always wanted to travel, go to parties and dance away all night. She had money. Aneesh was a salaried person. Since he had a fixed schedule each day, going to bed early and waking up early had been one of his top priorities. It wasn't long before there were clashes. It looked difficult to live together and follow radically different lifestyles under the same roof. She wondered if she was happy living as she was. She was perhaps professionally the most successful woman in her field. After so many years of leading separate lives, she did miss Aneesh.

She had never heard of any woman in Aneesh's life. An ideal husband, she thought and smiled to herself.

******

Shankar and Sanjeev were discussing a project in Sanjeev's cabin, when Ayesha entered. She was holding a copy of *The Grass*. She said triumphantly, 'There's something strange in this book.'

Sanjeev looked at her enquiringly.

'I just glanced through the manuscript. It has thirty chapters. Whereas this book, the printed one, has thirty-one chapters.'

'What is so surprising? During editing, a lengthy chapter might have been split into two.'

'No. It isn't like that. In fact, up to Chapter 30, everything is the same. An additional chapter, the last one, was inserted at a later stage.'

'You mean the climax has been changed?'

'Yes. In fact, it seems unnecessary. It has become a sort of an anticlimax.'

'How?' asked Shankar.

'Read it,' Ayesha offered, opened the book and placed it before Shankar.

Shankar went through Chapter 31 as well as Chapter 30. He looked up, frowning, when he had finished reading.

'You're right, Ayesha. It's not necessary. In fact, it goes against the basic storyline.'

Chapter 31

Sanjeev remarked, 'We're looking at it from a publisher's angle. The author might've found it interesting. He might've thought it would attract more readership.'

Both Ayesha and Shankar looked at each other. Ayesha turned to Sanjeev, 'This seems to have been added purposefully.'

'Purposefully?' Sanjeev repeated, puzzled.

'I'm not sure. No professional editor will do this. It wasn't there in the original manuscript. It's inexplicable.'

Shankar said, 'You could show it to Sheela Ma'am.'

'Yeah, but today she's gone to Hyderabad.'

'Send her an email.'

Sanjeev said, 'She isn't very particular in checking her emails.'

'So, what? Let Ayesha send the email.'

'Okay. Send it. Sheela Ma'am will forward it to Anand,' Sanjeev said sarcastically.

As Ayesha left Sanjeev's cabin, her mind was racing. What purpose could Chapter 31 possibly serve?

******

Sujata was quite annoyed with uncle's behaviour. Unable to control herself any longer, she finally burst out at Ashutosh.

'This is terrible, to put it mildly. We had full trust on uncle and look how he has betrayed us.'

'No, no, it's not like that. In fact, he was helping us in editing and promoting,' Ashutosh pointed out, loyally supporting his uncle. 'Well, yes, he could have told us at that time the reason behind inserting that chapter.'

'We're are fools,' Sujata continued ranting. 'We should have asked him as to why he gave his email address. He gave *his* email address in the book … he asked you not to get your photograph printed … he kept you in the dark all along!'

'Look, Sujata, he isn't a bad person. Uncle told us that his American colleague had told him to track the ex-chief of NCB. This isn't something illegal.' He poured out two glasses of water, one for himself and the other for Sujata. He set down her glass next to her on the side table. He sat down, stretched out his legs and sipped from his own glass.

Sujata looked at Ashutosh sadly. She said slowly, 'Ashutosh, you are so naive. Did you believe everything that uncle told you?'

'Is there a reason not to believe?'

'There might be some other reason. I'm not taking uncle for granted. You were his favourite. What he did is absolutely unacceptable. I still think there is something larger than what he has divulged.'

'Larger?'

'Yeah.'

'Now, you're making presumptions.'

'Who knows if they wanted to reach the minister or that so-called Paul. Contacting Mr Mehra may be step one. My only concern is that we've been dragged into all this,' Sujata said bitterly.

'Please, be calm.'

'I'm telling you, the world is complex. We're simple, peace-loving people. We don't want to be involved in any sort of controversy.'

'See, I can talk to uncle again.'

'Of what use will that be now, Ashutosh? The damage is already been done,' Sujata snorted in annoyance.

Ashutosh sighed; Sujata was right, he thought. She had been telling him all these weeks that there must be a reason why uncle was taking such keen interest in promoting and marketing his book. He had been blind. He hadn't figured out how a first-time writer could become a bestselling author. It was impossible.

Chapter 31

'By the way, I'll be going to Sana's house this Sunday,' Sujata broke his reverie, changing the subject.

'Okay,' Ashutosh said. Sana was Sujata's schoolmate.

'It's an all-women's gathering. Sana is pregnant and there is a baby shower on Sunday evening.'

'You mean you're going alone.'

'Of course,' Sujata said, laughing.

'You look nice when you laugh,' Ashutosh said, relieved that she was back to her usual happy self.

But Sujata was halfway into their bedroom, and didn't catch his last sentence.

******

They got down at Hyderabad airport.

'May I drop you somewhere?' Aneesh asked Sheela.

'No, they will have sent a car,' Sheela said.

They walked silently towards the exit. Sheela said, 'We could meet in Delhi someday.'

'That depends on you,' Aneesh looked straight into her eyes.

Sheela glanced at him and said, 'I'll phone you.'

'I'll wait.'

They said their goodbyes and went their respective ways.

As her phone pinged, Sheela looked at her mobile phone. There was an email from Ayesha. Without bothering to look at it, she forwarded it to Anand.

Chapter – 14

Anand read the email that Sheela had sent him. It was a forward that Ayesha had sent to Sheela:

Dear Ma'am,

I was going through the original manuscript of 'The Grass' that had been sent to Scholars. It had thirty chapters. The printed book has thirty-one chapters. Chapters 1 to 30 have a common thread. Chapter 31 seems to have been inserted at a later date. The contents of this chapter are a misfit with the rest of the book and it is unnecessary. I showed it to Sanjeev and Shankar. It may not be of much importance but I was advised to bring this to your knowledge.

Have a nice day.

Warm regards,

Ayesha

Anand picked up the book and read Chapter 31 again. On first reading, he hadn't found it to be unusual but now he agreed with Ayesha that it was a misfit. The complete plot of the novel, from Chapter 1 to Chapter 30, was well intertwined and the climax in Chapter 30, was a reasonable and well-deserved ending with the detention of the people involved and the confiscation of the drugs. The release of the suspects on the order of a minister by the NCB chief in the last chapter wasn't required. There was an unnecessary presence of a white man named Paul. The contents of that chapter on a whole looked meaningless.

He poured out a cup of coffee and reread Chapter 31. No, Anand frowned thinking deeply, it isn't meaningless. It has been done on purpose and the book has been marketed

Chapter 31

and popularized. That might've been done artificially. Well, what could be the purpose?

He had spent so many years reading books and the events narrated always had continuity with a view to engross the reader. It should be gripping. Likewise, a reader should remain interested till the end of *The Grass*. The end came in Chapter 30. A reader wouldn't expect three new characters in the last chapter.

******

It was 7 p.m. The weather was pleasant. Aneesh wasn't a habitual drinker but being a diplomat and posted in external affairs, he was expected to meet foreign nationals, particularly Russians. He was instrumental in giving shape to the foreign policies of the government, as well as ensuring that these were executed properly. It required considerable diplomatic skill, patience and knowledge of the economic, cultural and political background of the other country. He had told Sheela that he was to meet the Russian cultural delegation. Well, a cultural delegation was there but, in that delegation, Peter Avilov was one person who had nothing to do with culture. He was one of the employees of the Russian Ministry of External Affairs (MEA) and Aneesh had met him once on an earlier occasion. This time, he was visiting India as a member of that cultural delegation. He had expressed his desire to meet Aneesh on some urgent matter.

Aneesh entered the hotel lobby and asked for directions to the coffee shop, where he was to meet Peter Avilov. Peter was already at the coffee shop, waiting for him. He got up when he saw Aneesh coming towards him. They shook hands and sat down. The usual greetings were exchanged. This was a meeting between two diplomats. They were used to such meetings behind the curtain, through unofficial channels. A waiter approached their table; he served them two cups of coffee and a plate of savouries and departed.

'You came as a member of a cultural delegation?' Aneesh asked.

'Yes, to avoid unnecessary attention,' Peter said.

Aneesh smiled and said, 'Something important?'

'Part of the job. One has to come.'

Peter's English accent was far better than most of the Russians Aneesh had met.

'Tell me, what brings you to India?' Aneesh asked, sipping his coffee.

'Elections will soon be held in the US. The campaigns are in full swing. There are two main contenders: Paul Johnson and Sarah Baker. Our government is interested in Paul Johnson becoming the next president of the USA.' Peter's expression was as impassive as Aneesh's.

'According to our sources, it is highly likely that he will be the next president,' Aneesh said.

'You're right. Our government has also put in a lot of money in his campaigns.'

'Is it so? That's news.'

'Paul himself has a lot of money but still one wants to take no chances.' Peter set down his cup as he tried to gauge how much Aneesh knew about the dynamics at play here.

Aneesh was fully aware of the developments in the US and also of Russia's interest. He asked, 'Why is your government so keen that Paul must win?'

'That's a policy matter. You know, we're told to execute. We're employees,' a hint of a smile hovered on Peter's lips for a few seconds. 'We're to just ensure that the policy gets implemented and if there's some hindrance, the same has to be resolved.'

'Yes, of course. We have to,' Aneesh acknowledged.

Chapter 31

'Obviously.'

'So, what can we do? I mean, our government.'

'The American intelligence agencies are favouring Sarah. They're also playing all sorts of tricks. The elections are still six months away. You know, Steve, the CIA chief, will leave no stone unturned.'

Aneesh was aware of this. Sarah was Steve's favourite.

'But it's public opinion that matters and not Steve's opinion,' Aneesh pointed out, flicking away a crumb that had fallen on his jacket.

'You know very well that Steve is capable of reversing public opinion.'

'You're right but the public isn't foolish.'

Peter looked at Aneesh intently and said slowly, 'We've inputs from our intelligence sources that Steve is digging into Paul's past and if he gets anything against him, it will be damaging.'

'Do you think Paul's past may have something so damaging?'

'Everyone has a buried past. If Steve gets hold of any loose ends …'

'Look, Peter, tell me clearly. We're here to talk straight. What are you expecting? What is your fear?'

Peter was quiet for a brief while, and then said, 'Paul Johnson used to run a drug racket.'

'Narcotics?'

'Yes. That's what our sources suggest but he closed all those operations before he joined politics,' Peter said as he wiped his mouth with his napkin.

'That's interesting.'

'Paul was a clever operator. He was born and brought up in Latin America. There used to be clandestine cultivation of opium. He was smart. At a young age he came to North America and the opium business was continued by others. He was the master operator but he was careful not to be in the front and not to be caught. He didn't leave any evidence of his being in narcos. With the money he made, he expanded his hotel business and retail store business. He kept his record clear. He had established a distribution network all over the world. At a later stage, when he made up his mind to join politics, he left narcos altogether because he knew that politics and narcos cannot go together.'

Aneesh was listening. He had also heard the rumours. He said to Peter, 'Steve must be aware of all this.'

'Definitely. But in the absence of any evidence, he's helpless. He's desperate to find something against Paul.'

'Now I understand. Your concerns are genuine. One clue and Paul is gone.'

'Not exactly but it would definitely cause substantial damage. It depends on how strong the evidence would be – if he could lay hands on any.'

'Yes, it would all depend on the evidence, if any,' Aneesh said thoughtfully. He was still waiting for Peter to reveal further.

Peter said, 'Our intelligence agencies has intercepted some messages.'

'What messages?' Aneesh asked, all ears.

'Once – long time ago – a consignment of drugs and five men were caught by the NCB here in India. The men were stated to be released at the intervention of a politician.'

'Our politician?'

'Yes. The CIA is looking for a lead. One of their agents is here. As per the intercepted messages, he's in touch with one Rahul Mehra, perhaps an ex-chief of NCB. The agent is pursuing Mr Mehra and might be able to extract something from him. We're not sure. It was long ago. Mr Mehra may, at the most, narrate the whole incident. But that's his word against anybody's. Nobody is going to take that seriously.'

Chapter 31

'Then why are you worried?'

'What if he has something against Paul?'

'Very, very remote. I know the working of our officers. They may be honest. They may be loyal. They may be hard-working. They may be fearless. But once retired, they've retired.'

'That sounds assuring. You see, I've been sent to request you to stop Rahul Mehra from handing over anything to the American agent, anything which could jeopardize Paul becoming the next US president.'

Aneesh had faced such situations in his career a number of times. He said, 'Peter, it's the policy of our government not to interfere in elections being held in any other country.'

'I'm not asking you to interfere or influence the election. That's what we are doing,' Peter said and smiled. He continued, 'I'm just asking for a small favour that this gentleman – Rahul Mehra – has to be stopped. He lives somewhere in Delhi.'

'Okay. Let me first find out who Rahul Mehra is and where he lives.'

'And also, to find out whether he is in possession of some evidence.'

'Sure. I will.'

'I shall be thankful. Our government shall be thankful,' Peter said simply.

They finished the meeting. Peter gave Aneesh his contact number for any further details.

Aneesh came out of the hotel. So, Russia wanted Paul to be the next president of the USA. Russia had an apprehension that Steve had something up his sleeve. It would be amazing if Russia were able to see the candidate of their choice become the next president of the USA. Public opinion was being built up, favouring Paul. Aneesh thought if he tried to stop Rahul, it would definitely catch the attention of the Americans. According to Peter, they had already tracked Rahul and he was sure to be under strict surveillance. India wouldn't like to antagonize the US. At the same time, it wasn't advisable to refuse Peter's 'request'. A balance would have to be maintained.

Aneesh was heading towards the airport as he had to be back in Delhi that day itself. His thoughts kept drifting to his conversation with Peter. He kept pondering how that information could be used to India's advantage. First, he would have to find out who was Rahul Mehra, which he thought would not be difficult. He had another option of not taking Peter seriously right now and wait. There was still time and it wasn't the opportune moment to react to Peter's request. It would be interesting to see how desperate Peter would get.

Chapter – 15

Anand was sitting in Sheela's cabin. He told her that Ayesha's observation of the mismatch between the manuscript and the printed book was significant. He also told her that had he edited the manuscript with the thirty-first chapter, he would have advised deleting the last chapter but it had actually been the other way round. The chapter had been inserted and this had distorted the storyline. Sheela listened to him, leaning back in her chair.

Ayesha entered Sheela's cabin.

'Good morning,' Ayesha wished them pleasantly.

'Good morning,' Anand replied, smiling.

'How are you, sir?'

'I'm good! We were just discussing the email you sent yesterday.'

'Isn't it strange?'

'Definitely. It's something that demands our attention, we have to understand the reason behind it.'

Sheela interrupted, 'What for? We're in publishing. This is not our product.'

'But you're considering publishing it under the Spellers brand,' Anand reminded her.

'Yes, I am. Why, at this stage, should we be unnecessarily concerned?'

'It's out of curiosity, Sheela,' Anand said, opening the palms of his hand in exasperation.

'Ayesha, I called you to ask you to brief me about the contents of the last chapter. Be brief.' Sheela instructed her junior in a crisp tone.

Ayesha summarized the chapter briefly. Sheela was perhaps listening to a storyline for the first time.

When Ayesha finished, Sheela asked, 'You mean, there's no mention of any of the three characters – the minister, Umesh Kumar and Paul – in any of the previous chapters.'

'Nowhere,' Anand said. 'They appear for the first time in the last chapter and that is where the novel ends.'

'You see, I never go through the contents of a novel much. But yes, it looks out of place,' Sheela agreed.

Anand resumed, 'My feeling is that the book has been promoted and marketed only for the last chapter to reach the intended person.'

'What do you mean "intended person"?'

'Any of the three?' Anand suggested.

'Nonsense! Why would anyone go to that extent to find a person? There are a lot of simple methods to do that,' Sheela scoffed.

Ayesha said slowly, 'Have we been able to find Ashutosh, the author, by using those "simple methods"?'

There was pin-drop silence for a moment.

'She's right. Sometimes, it's difficult, and it becomes even *more* difficult in the face of a larger conspiracy,' Anand said.

Sheela said abruptly, 'Enough on this book. Let's talk about other books. We should concentrate on our pending projects.'

Ayesha nodded and left Sheela's cabin.

Sheela looked at Anand and said, 'More knowledge is sometimes dangerous. My one and only concern was that the book, being one of the bestsellers, should have come to us because so far, it's being self-published. There's no publisher. It's easier at this stage. We've published numerous novels and you have perhaps read all of them. Have we ever scrutinized the contents of any book so minutely?'

Chapter 31

'You're right. I think we're unnecessarily analysing the contents. Such discussion is outside the scope of our profession.'

'Exactly!' Sheela said and they switched to other topics.

******

It was 3 p.m. when Sarah Baker came out of the small airport located at the outskirts of Washington D.C. She was accompanied by two of her poll managers. These two took care of Sarah's campaign schedule and her speeches would also be vetted by them. That day, she would be speaking to the students of Georgetown University at 5 p.m. Sarah requested her managers to go to the university to oversee and check the arrangement there, and in the meanwhile she would meet her relative. She told them that she would reach the venue before the scheduled time.

A chauffeur-driven car was waiting for her and she got into it. As the car sped to its destination, Sarah looked outside. It was a sunny day. She knew the roads and lanes of Washington D.C. as she had completed her school education in this city, and thereafter had completed her graduation and postgraduation from Stanford University.

As she took in the city view, her thoughts drifted to the meeting ahead. Steve had told her that it would take her half an hour to reach and that the meeting wouldn't last more than half an hour.

The car entered a hospital compound. The hospital building was oval in shape. The car moved along the right loop of the road. After a couple of minutes, it moved towards a lane on the right side and stopped at the driveway. There were two guards on duty, one of whom came forward, opened the car door and escorted Sarah inside the building. As she entered, she saw an old man sitting in an old-fashioned chair. It was Steve; he was the chief of the CIA. Everyone referred to him as Steve. Sarah was meeting him in person for the first time. She had heard that Steve wasn't in the habit of meeting people, in general.

'Good afternoon, sir,' Sarah said.

'Good afternoon,' Steve reciprocated and gestured that she should sit in the chair that had been placed opposite his; it seemed as if it had been specifically placed for her. She sat down. Sarah had also been told that Steve didn't speak much. He spoke only as many words as needed to get the point across.

'How is the campaigning going on?'

'Good, sir.'

'Can I say, I'm talking to the future president?'

Sarah grew serious and said slowly, 'Sir, I'm using all my resources. I'm trying my best.'

'Do you think your limited resources, your unimpeachable reputation and your well-researched speeches are sufficient to win this election?' Steve asked.

She kept quiet.

Steve continued, 'You know the answer. I don't have to tell you that your winning the elections is essential for the country.'

Sarah remained silent.

Steve said, 'I have a suggestion. From tomorrow onwards, you will use a sentence in your speeches and debates.'

As Sarah tilted her head, looking at him enquiringly, Steve replied firmly, 'That Paul Johnson is a drug racketeer.'

'What!? No, I can't do that!' Sarah exclaimed, taken aback.

'You're scared that Paul may sue you.'

'Yes, definitely!'

'No,' Steve said, smiling grimly. 'He will not.'

'Sir, I can't say that sentence publicly without any evidence. It would be suicidal.'

Chapter 31

'*You* know that you don't have the evidence, but Paul doesn't know that. He won't file a suit against you because he'll think you have not made the statement without evidence, particularly in presidential elections, which are of utmost importance.'

Sarah stood up and said politely but firmly, 'Sir, I'll now take your leave. I'm sorry, I'll not say that.'

Steve placed his hands on the arms of his chair, lowered his head, thought for a moment and slowly got up. He walked towards Sarah and came to where she was standing. He placed his right hand on her shoulder and smiled.

'Suppose there's some news in a local newspaper somewhere in the middle pages ... can you quote that in your speeches or debates?' Steve asked.

Sarah thought for a couple of minutes and nodded her head in affirmation. Steve stepped aside so that she could leave. As she was about to go out of the room, Steve said crisply, 'Tomorrow morning you'll get the newspaper with the news marked for you.'

Sarah came out and got into the car, her mind in a whirl. She mulled over Steve's advice and decided that quoting from a newspaper would be no problem. It wouldn't affect her reputation adversely and Paul would have to defend himself against the report and against that newspaper. She couldn't be implicated for making a false or derogatory statement against her opponent. She looked at her watch. The time was 4.15 p.m. and she would reach the venue on time.

Steve, on the other hand, knew that a small news item, when quoted by a candidate of the Democratic Party, would become headlines in all newspapers. He was more interested in the reactions of all who were supporting Paul, particularly those who were funding him from outside the USA through multiple channels. He would take the next step after observing those reactions. Steve didn't have any evidence in his hands except Rahul Mehra's words, as narrated to him by Justin. He had heard the recording of the conversation between the two, which Justin had forwarded to him. He had asked Justin to keep a watch on Rahul Mehra's movements.

******

Aneesh had decided not to respond to Peter but he wanted to find out about Rahul and in this matter, he asked his staff to take the help of those in the intelligence field. He was sure that he would get all the information within an hour because Rahul had been in government service and all records would be available. It wouldn't be difficult. However, after three hours, what his staff informed him was surprising. One Rahul Mehra had been the chief of NCB about ten years ago. He had suddenly disappeared and no one knew about his whereabouts. It wasn't even known whether he was dead or alive or had migrated to some other country.

How is that possible? he thought. Then he remembered Peter telling him that Rahul lived somewhere in Delhi and that American intelligence personnel had traced Rahul and established contact with him. How come he isn't on government records? Aneesh pondered, surprised.

There was a knock on his door. He said, 'Come in.'

It was a clerk who had come to give him a file. Seeing Aneesh absent-minded, he enquired, 'All well, sir?'

'Oh, yes, yes,' Aneesh said. 'Tell me, if someone was in government service, and has retired, what is the way to find his address?'

'Very simple. He must be drawing a pension. Just ask the pension office and they'll tell you the bank and account number where the pension is being credited every month.'

'You're a genius!' beamed Aneesh.

The clerk smiled and said modestly, 'Sir, these are small things, which don't occur to senior people like you.'

Chapter – 16

The ghost of the past, which had been buried years ago, was now coming out of its grave. Rahul had never anticipated that that affair would become important after ten years. The minister's cook had spilled the beans to Justin. What had happened on the previous day and the next day was unknown to the world. He recollected.

******

On the day of the seizure of drugs, his officers had brought the drugs, the car, the two laptops and the five men to office. The five men were made to sit in separate rooms for questioning. The two men who had come to deliver the drugs had named Paul. The last name Johnson was neither told nor was known to them. He was simply known as 'Paul' in the drug trade. They were questioned about the two laptops, which had been seized from the car. The officers couldn't open the laptops as these were password protected; and it was essential to know the passwords as without these they would be unable to access the files in the laptops. The two men to whom the laptops belonged were not ready to cooperate; they had refused to divulge the password. They kept repeating that they were not aware of the passwords. The officers had informed Rahul Mehra, their chief. Rahul had told them to get hold of the passwords somehow. It was important. Rahul hadn't entered any of the rooms; he hadn't seen any of the accused. He was certain his officers would be able to extract the passwords. This wasn't the first time that they were faced with such a challenge.

Rahul was sitting in his cabin, somewhat relaxed. Unlocking a laptop had never been a problem. The NCB had the authority to send it to the topmost technological institute of the country, who would unlock it officially. It wasn't a matter of concern. He had directed his officers to record the statement of the three men who were taking the delivery because their role was limited only to the extent of receiving the drugs. The statements of the other two could wait till they started talking.

At about 8 p.m., when he was about to leave his office, the minister's assistant called and informed Rahul that the minister wanted to meet him at 7.30 a.m. the next day. That was the only message, and it was nothing new. Rahul was used to such things. Whenever a big case was underway, strings would be pulled behind the scenes and efforts made to dilute the case on hand. Rahul Mehra, the chief of NCB, was an expert in dealing with these situations.

Next morning, when he visited the minister's residence, he couldn't have imagined that the kingpin of the trade, Paul, would be there, and having breakfast with the minister. Whatever happened at the minister's residence has been narrated in the last chapter of *The Grass*. The cook had narrated almost all in detail.

Rahul was still in a state of shock when he entered his office after his meeting with the minister. Never before had the nexus been made as obvious as the minister had made it that morning. He had spoken and instructed him in front of Paul and hadn't made any effort to conceal Paul's identity. In fact, the minister had clearly indicated, 'Look, how close we are.' Another shocking part of the minister's direction was his order to release the accused people. Rahul had the reputation of an honest, loyal and strict officer. Once an information was received, he would ensure till the end that the case was meticulously built, irrespective of the pressures. His officers too worked under him cheerfully because they always felt protected. They knew that their boss was there to absorb all the adverse

Chapter 31

impacts. This time, the minister himself came to the front to save his 'friend'. That was strange. Normally, in such a situation, when a case had been prepared, powerful men dissociated themselves from the accused, though indirectly they did try to manipulate events.

Lalit Gaur, one of the intelligence officers, knocked on the door and entered Rahul's cabin. Lalit's eyes were red, he looked tired. He must have questioned the accused the whole night.

'Good morning, sir.'

'Good morning,' Rahul said and asked him to sit down.

'Sir, one of the two men has finally cracked and revealed the password and we have unlocked one of the laptops. We still don't have the password of the other one. We feel neither of them knows it.'

'So, you were successful in accessing one of the laptops,' Rahul observed, joining the tips of the fingers of both hands. 'Is there anything of importance?'

'Yes, sir. The emails relate to the delivery of drugs, the schedule, the quantity to be delivered and the money negotiated.'

'Do the emails mention a "Paul" anywhere?'

'At a number of places,' confirmed Lalit. 'In most places, "under the direction of Paul" has been mentioned.'

'What else?'

'There's a folder with details of names and addresses of the people involved throughout India. There is another folder, which has similar details relating to people in Thailand and Malaysia.'

'Good work, Lalit. Have you confronted these people?'

'Yes. They're ready to admit everything.'

Rahul thought for a while and asked, 'How many of you stayed back last night?'

'Five of us, sir. Gagan, Satish, Hanif and Vijay are also there.'

'All are here now?'

'Yes, sir.'

'Tell all of them to come to my cabin now. It's urgent.'

'Sure, sir.'

Lalit left and in another ten minutes, all five were sitting with Rahul.

Rahul knew that all these five hand-picked officers were faithful to him. He could trust them. That day he would be telling them something they would never have expected to hear. Rahul looked at each of them and told them everything about the meeting he had had with the minister that morning. He made no attempt to hide anything. He told them explicitly that Paul was sitting there and the minister had unashamedly introduced him. He told them that the minister had ordered the release of everything – the drugs, the men and the laptops. He managed to stop the release of the drugs but the minister was adamant that the men be released and laptops returned.

All the officers, tired after spending a sleepless gruelling night, listened, stunned into silence. Finally, Rahul told them, 'I leave it to you – all of you. You decide.'

They looked at each other, speechless. They had been working on this case for the last six months. They never wanted it to become a failure.

Lalit looked at Rahul and said, 'Sir, can we disobey the minister's orders?'

'Nothing is in writing, Lalit. If you decide not to release them, I'm with you. I will bear the brunt, don't worry on that account,' Rahul said quietly.

'Suppose, sir, they tried to shoot us or we weren't armed and they were successful in getting away, we would have come back with the drugs and made an unclaimed seizure.'

Chapter 31

Rahul smiled sadly and sighed, 'You needn't be that faithful. You're just trying to convince yourself – or consoling yourself.'

'Yes, sir. But we know the consequence of antagonizing a minister. They're all powerful. One can fight anyone but not them,' Hanif said.

The other four echoed Hanif's statement.

'For me, it has become a difficult situation. On one side, this is a clear case, you've been able to unlock one of the laptops. The men are ready to admit all the details in the laptop. On the other side, there's this minister ...' Rahul trailed off.

'Sir, we're the servants. The minister stands for "Government". We're bound to obey,' Lalit remarked.

Rahul suddenly asked them, 'Have you all had breakfast?'

'Yes, sir. We'd ordered some food to be delivered here at the office itself,' Gagan said.

'Okay, good. Let me go through the whole situation once more and I'll let you know, say, in an hour.'

As the five officers stood up to leave, Rahul said to Lalit, 'There's something more that I want to discuss with you.'

When the other officers left, Rahul said, 'We've one hour. Record the statement of the person who is ready to admit. Finish it in an hour's time. We've no option but to release them.'

'Right, sir.'

'And one more thing, Lalit. Copy all the relevant files in the laptop into a pen drive.'

'I'll do that, sir,' Lalit nodded.

'Don't copy anything in front of those men.'

After one hour, the statements of four men – three prospective recipients and one of the two deliverers – were before him. The seizure memo of the drugs was also there.

The accused were allowed to go and the laptops were returned. The matter was closed. Rahul asked all five to go home and rest. Lalit handed over a pen drive to him. Rahul leant back in his chair, trying to absorb the shock. He was feeling extremely guilty that day. He had never felt so helpless before.

Two days passed uneventfully. On the third day, he was summoned to the minister's office with the case file. Rahul went to the minister's cabin, file in hand, knowing fully well that the file he was carrying with him wouldn't come back with him. Before leaving for the meeting, he asked his assistant Malini to take photocopies. When he reached the minister's cabin, he was asked for the case file.

The minister glanced through the papers and said, 'I told you the other day, not to keep anything, why are these statements here?'

'Sir, these men were detained at our office the whole night. My staff was doing a routine exercise of questioning and recording of statements. They didn't know that they would be asked to release them. I took these papers from them.'

'Good. Leave these papers with me.'

The minister opened his drawer and handed over an envelope and an official passport which had a white cover. He told Rahul, 'I appreciate your cooperation. Here is your official passport and the envelope which contains your order. You're posted at the Indian High Commission in London. Report there by tomorrow. Buy a business class ticket. The fare is reimbursable,' the minister smiled and continued, 'this is a token of my regard for you. You see, everyone wants to be posted in European countries.'

Before Rahul could say anything, the minister said, watching him attentively, 'All the best.' And extended his hand.

Chapter 31

This was another bolt from the blue. Rahul had seen in the course of his tenure in government service that a posting abroad was sometimes given not as prize posting but simply because the person concerned should be sent abroad in order to cut him off from his fellow colleagues. These postings were for five years and when the person would return after their tenure, the dust would have settled. The minister simply wanted Rahul to be away from NCB. The objective was that Rahul shouldn't talk about this particular episode with anyone, especially with his own circle of civil servants.

When he came out of the minister's cabin, he passed through the minister's assistant's cabin. The assistant greeted Rahul, even as Rahul glanced at the passport. He observed that the first name was 'Rakul' and not 'Rahul'. It seemed to be a typing error. Instead of the letter H, the letter K had been printed. He opened the envelope.

The order also mentioned the name 'Rakul Mehra'. He turned around and went back to the minister's cabin. The minister looked up when he knocked and entered his cabin.

'Yes?'

'Sir, there seems to be some error. My name is Rahul but the posting order and the passport show "Rakul".'

'It's not an error. It has been deliberately done,' the minister informed him, leaning back in his chair, his hands placed lightly on his rotund belly.

'Why, sir?'

'I don't know. It was done on the suggestion of the intelligence people. It seems having a passport in a different name is common with them.'

'But …'

'Don't worry. You're being posted to the high commission. Nobody is going to question you. You're holding an official passport issued *officially*.'

That was how those three days had passed and after those three days, Rahul Mehra disappeared.

******

Aneesh was informed by the pension office that there was no person by the name of Rahul Mehra availing the pension. It was strange. This would be the case when a government employee had expired, whereas according to Peter, Rahul Mehra was alive, living in Delhi and the Americans had been successful in contacting him. Both were contradictory situations. He had been certain that finding Rahul would be easy and he was right because it was easy to see the records of a government employee, whether serving or retired. He had, however, confirmed the information that the NCB did have a chief about ten years back by the name of Rahul Mehra. All leads thereafter were broken.

Chapter – 17

There was a mad rush of media personnel outside the hotel where Sarah Baker was staying. She had given a speech in a town hall meeting of Maryland that day. During the meeting, she had referred to a small news item that had appeared in a local newspaper published from Oakland, a county of Maryland. The news stated that Paul Johnson was a drug smuggler and that his entire business empire was based on money made from narcotics. In a very casual manner, at the end of the speech, she quoted the same. That came as a surprise to her media manager too because he hadn't been taken into confidence beforehand. The contents of the speech were normally vetted by him. Sarah never deviated from what was briefed to her but on that day her reference to this particular news carried in a local newspaper was out of context.

Soon after the speech, she returned to the hotel where she was to stay overnight. The news spread like fire. The media, both digital and print, had gathered outside the hotel and wanted to talk to Sarah. She called her media manager inside and gave him a short, written statement. She told him to go outside and announce to the media that she had only that much to say. The statement read:

> I haven't made any allegation against my contender. I know him personally. He is a gentle and humble person. I've only referred to a news item that appeared in the media and I hope that the same may be proved false.

Her media manager read it aloud to the media people who were hanging around outside the hotel, and distributed copies of this short statement to them. Gradually, the media dispersed.

******

There was a call on Aneesh's unlisted number. He picked up the phone. It was Peter.

'Hello?' came Peter's voice at the other end.

'Yes, good evening.'

'Did you hear?'

'What?' Aneesh asked.

'Sarah Baker, in a speech at Maryland, has stated that Paul Johnson was a drug smuggler.'

'Is that so? It's nowhere on the Indian media.'

'Soon it will travel to you.'

'You called me to tell me this?'

'Yes. I had my apprehensions. I suggested to you that day that you should find out about Rahul Mehra and stop him from going to the American intelligence.' Peter sounded displeased.

'Has she named Rahul Mehra?'

'No, she has simply referred to some news item. It was an indirect reference. That's how it's done ... such serious allegations are never made directly. These are leaked to the media first. There must be some background. You know the drill!'

'You're right.'

'If she gets hold of some solid information, it would cause irreparable loss. You *have* to stop Rahul Mehra. Before things acquire a larger magnitude.'

'Are you sure that the name is Rahul Mehra?'

'Yes. What happened?'

'I've gone through the records, checked them. There's no Rahul Mehra.'

'It *is* Rahul Mehra. Please act fast. He was the chief of NCB at that time.'

'*That* is correct. He *was* the chief of NCB at that time but there's no record thereafter.'

Chapter 31

'I'm telling you he is there somewhere in Delhi … and an American agent has contacted him,' Peter sounded exasperated.

'Okay. I'll get more inputs and apprise you.'

'Please do. I'll wait.'

As Peter disconnected the call, Aneesh smiled. Now Peter was getting desperate. He was in a position to strike a deal with the Russians. But it was important to talk to Rahul first. American intelligence had been able to find an Indian citizen here in India itself and the Government of India was unable to find the same person in its own territory! Aneesh called the Home Department and asked them to put efficient officers to locate the whereabouts of Rahul Mehra. It was urgent.

******

Next day, the small news item in the local newspaper became a headline across national newspapers: *IS PAUL JOHNSON A DRUG SMUGGLER?*

The news spread all over the world. It was front page news in the newspapers of other countries too.

Steve had read four newspapers since morning. The small news brief had its desired effect. Now he would wait and watch Paul's reaction as well as that of his supporters and the Russians. He had asked his agent to remain on alert. He had, however, asked Justin to wait: Justin was to just keep a watch on Rahul.

******

Twenty-two women had gathered at Sana's house, for her baby shower. Sana was an old friend of Sujata's. Sana's mother, mother-in-law, her sister, aunties and a few friends were there. They had brought gifts for the baby to be born.

Certain rituals were performed. Sana was made to sit in a chair. One-by-one the women came up to her and placed their gifts in her lap. After the completion of rituals, there was much singing, dancing, laughter, joking and feasting.

Sujata was sitting with Sana, when Sana suddenly asked her, 'When are you planning?'

'Planning what?'

'A baby, silly.'

Sujata laughed and said, 'It's a huge responsibility.'

'The sooner, the better,' Sana spouted wisely.

'You're right, but there's still time.'

Meanwhile Sana's sister, who had been attending to the guests, came and sat down with them. Sana introduced them, 'Sujata, my sister,' Sana gestured towards her sister.

'Hello,' Sujata smiled.

'Pleasure meeting you,' the sister replied, politely, smiling.

'We haven't met before.'

'Were you not there at Sana's wedding?' Sana's sister asked curiously.

'No, I was out of town. I missed it.' The regret in Sujata's tone made the sisters smile.

Two hours passed by and the women started leaving. Sujata, too, bid farewell to Sana, hugged her and was about to leave, when Sana's sister saw *The Grass* lying beside Sana. She asked Sana casually, 'Who brought it?' nodding at it.

'Sujata,' Sana replied, gently lowering herself into the couch. 'You know, Sujata's husband has written this book and it's become quite popular. She brought a copy for me.'

Sana's sister exclaimed, 'Where's Sujata?'

'She just left ... in front of you. Why? What happened?'

Without replying, Sana's sister picked up the book and ran outside; she saw Sujata sitting in her car, about to drive

Chapter 31

off. She waved at Sujata to stop, shouting out her name simultaneously.

'Yes?' Sujata asked, surprised, taking in the excited face.

'Your husband has written this?' Sana's sister asked, breathlessly, waving *The Grass* at her.

'Yeah.'

'Ashutosh?' The young girl could hardly believe her luck.

'Yeah. Do you know him?' Sujata wondered at her eagerness.

'No, but would like to meet him. Where is he?' she replied, trying to compose herself, as she noticed Sujata's expression.

'At home.'

'May I come with you?'

'It would be a pleasure,' Sujata said politely.

'One second, please. I'll just tell Sana I'm going to your place.'

In another thirty minutes, both of them were at Sujata's house.

Ashutosh opened the door when the doorbell rang.

'Ashutosh, this beautiful young lady is excited to meet you. She's Sana's sister.'

'Please, do come inside,' Ashutosh welcomed her, and stepped aside for both the ladies to enter.

Sana's sister extended her hand and introduced herself, 'I'm Ayesha.'

Ashutosh shook her hand and said, 'Nice meeting you, Ayesha.'

Ayesha was thrilled and delighted at this stroke of luck. They sat down in the small living room.

Ayesha, still clutching The Grass in her hand, mumbled, 'Ashutosh … I …'

'Yes?'

'Oh, my God, Ashutosh, we've been looking for you for so many weeks now!'

'Why?' Puzzled, Ashutosh and Sujata exchanged glances.

'I'm the chief editor at Spellers.'

Ashutosh was surprised, and so was Sujata. Sana had never mentioned that her sister was with Spellers. Ayesha enthusiastically started telling the couple how the owner of Spellers had got interested in publishing this book, the effort the Spellers' staff had made to find the writer. Ashutosh listened with pleasure. It felt good to hear that the country's top publisher had been looking for him.

When she had finished bringing them up-to-date, Ayesha asked, 'Why didn't you reply to the email we sent you?'

'I didn't get any email. To which email address did you send it?'

Ayesha looked confused. 'The one mentioned in the book, of course.'

Ashutosh and Sujata looked at each other. It was uncle's email address. That meant uncle hadn't informed them.

'I might have missed it,' Ashutosh said, his excuse sounding rather lame to his own ears.

Feeling annoyed with uncle, Sujata excused herself and went into the kitchen to prepare tea for the three of them. She could hear Ayesha and Ashutosh talking animatedly about his book. 'You had sent the manuscript to Scholars at the initial stage.'

'Yes.'

'Scholars is our company's imprint which encourages first-time authors.'

'Yes, I know, but they demanded a lot of money.'

Chapter 31

Sujata entered the living room, carrying a tray with tea and a plate of biscuits. She set down the tray on the centre table, and requested them to help themselves.

As they settled down with their tea, Ayesha's eyes fell on the wall clock and, realizing that it was getting late, she excused herself and quickly booked a cab. That done, Ayesha smiled and said, 'You're right. That has become one more source to make money even by reputed publishers.'

'I'd sent it ... I don't exactly remember when ... but I'd received an auto reply. Then I didn't bother.'

'But how did you make it so popular? You're really lucky to write a book, self-publish it, and reach such a level. How did you manage that?' Ayesha asked, taking a biscuit.

'I don't know,' grinned Ashutosh. 'I simply wrote the book.'

'You mean, the promotion and marketing were done by someone else? See, books don't sell on their own. These have to be marketed like any other product. In the publishing industry, the cost of printing is much less than other expenses, which are double the cost of printing.'

Ashutosh looked at Sujata and didn't reply. He sipped his tea.

'Anyway, when I tell my colleagues tomorrow that I've met you, the author of *The Grass*, they'll be very happy,' Ayesha said.

'That's really nice to know.'

'Tell me about it!' Ayesha chuckled. 'Our Sheela Ma'am is interested in publishing this book. She may like to meet you.'

Ashutosh, undoubtedly, would have liked his book to be published by Spellers because it was a huge platform. This would also help him in getting any of his new work published. But he was in two minds because of the implications that they were now aware of, after their conversation with uncle. Sujata was also thinking on the same lines.

'You see, I'll have to talk to the person who has already invested a lot in the promotion and marketing of this book,' Ashutosh clarified.

Ayesha considered this and thought Ashutosh was right professionally. She said, 'That won't be a problem. You can talk to whoever they are. You can do one thing: sign a contract that you are engaging Spellers for publishing your book.'

'How's that possible?'

'Why not? You have the copyright. Spellers won't be able to publish without your consent. But there's one thing that we need: you see, the manuscript, which you sent to Scholars, has thirty chapters, whereas the printed book has thirty-one chapters. I'll have to ask you to send the complete manuscript consisting of all thirty-one chapters. In the absence of the same, we can't proceed. You have to sign a contract for future publishing rights and that future date cannot be prior to the date of your sending the complete manuscript.'

Both Ashutosh and Sujata were silent. There was no reason for any author not to accept an offer from Spellers. Ashutosh said, 'I'm grateful that you are taking a personal interest but I need to tell you something.'

But Ayesha got up abruptly as her mobile phone pinged. She looked at them apologetically and said, 'I'm afraid I'll have to rush now, my cab is here. Sujata, please tell your husband no ifs and buts. I'll talk to Sheela Ma'am and tomorrow I'll be back with a copy of the contract duly prepared as per your requirement. You can tell me whatever you have in mind tomorrow when I come. And believe me, I'm not obliging you. You're obliging me.'

Ayesha went out. Both Ashutosh and Sujata came out to see her off.

Chapter 31

Once Ayesha had left, they went back inside and Sujata turned to Ashutosh, 'Why were you behaving so weirdly?'

'What do you mean?' Ashutosh asked as he shut the door.

'It was such a good opportunity, Ashutosh, and you were hesitating.'

'Sujata, you heard that Spellers sent an email but uncle didn't inform us. He must have had some reason ... still, I'll talk to him before agreeing to Ayesha's proposal. I'll of course be extremely happy if *The Grass* is published by Spellers.'

'Uncle has got us into trouble by inserting the last chapter. If that chapter hadn't been added, you could have said yes right now.'

'Exactly. Let me talk to uncle tomorrow morning. I hope he won't mind,' Ashutosh said as he sat down at his desk, and started to browse through his lecture notes for the next day.

'Okay. I'll tell Ayesha not to come before evening.'

'Yes, do that. And I would like to tell her the background of the last chapter. I don't want to hide anything, if I'm to be associated with Spellers.'

'I agree,' Sujata replied, as she curled up in a sofa with the day's newspaper.

PART - III

Chapter – 18

A TV crew was at the residence of Paul Johnson, the candidate of the Republican Party. The crew had arranged their cameras, lights, microphones, wires, and the like. Paul was sitting in a chair, placed in the middle of the room and a senior journalist sat opposite him in another chair. On receiving the signal that he could proceed, the journalist began the interview, asking questions regarding Paul's views on armaments, threats from some of the Islamic countries, curbs on immigration, deportation of illegal immigrants, employment, import of oil and all such related issues. Paul replied confidently in a well-rehearsed manner. Finally, the journalist asked, 'Sir, there was a news item in the press today regarding your past – that you were dealing in drugs. Do you have anything to say?'

Paul was expecting this question. In fact, the purpose of the interview was to arrive at this subject.

'No, I've nothing to say,' Paul said.

'Sir, will you not deny it?'

'Certainly. I don't think it was fair on the part of the opponent candidate to make such a baseless statement.'

'Don't you think, sir, it will tarnish your image?'

'I think she's stooped very low while campaigning for a prestigious post. It lowers the status of the post for which we are contending. I too can make a similar statement, saying that Sarah Baker was a drug addict. But I wouldn't say, even if I know that she was a drug addict during her college days.'

'Sir, are you suggesting that she was a drug addict?'

'No. I never said it. I never suggested it. I don't believe in such negative campaigning. It has never occurred in the history of America's presidential campaigns.'

Chapter 31

'Will you sue her?'

'Has she made any allegations against me?' Paul Johnson smiled at him disarmingly.

'She says she was quoting a news article.'

'That's right. There's no question of my suing her. Moreover, I don't want to waste my time and energy on trivial matters.'

'Is there anything else you would like to add, sir?'

'No, that's all.'

'Thank you, sir, for giving us your valuable time.'

'Thank you,' Paul nodded, smiling broadly.

The cameras were switched off. Paul took out the microphone tucked in his shirt and handed it over to a member of the TV crew. He smiled at everyone, waved his hand and went into another room.

Paul was extremely worried. For the last four years, he had dissociated himself from the drug trade completely. In fact, none of his friends, party colleagues, managers and supporters had the slightest hint of his involvement in the drug trade all those years ago. Sarah mentioning his name was a bolt from the blue for him. Somebody must have put her up to it. The news article was just a facade. It was a planned attack on him. He was apprehensive because she might come up with something more. Though he had no police record anywhere in the world, it could definitely damage his reputation as well as his chances of becoming the next president. Things were favourable for him at the moment.

He had a major problem on his hands now. None of his present associates were aware of his past. Naturally, he couldn't ask them to find out what was happening behind the curtain. His old associates in the drug trade could be helpful, though. Those associates had a wide network of their own and were in a position to ascertain the source of Sarah's knowledge. But he couldn't contact them. One wrong move would ruin everything. It was likely that he was under the surveillance of the CIA or other similar agencies. One of his poll managers had apprised him that the CIA was not in favour of his becoming the US president. Admittedly, he had no evidence that the CIA was supporting Sarah. After pondering over it for a long time, he decided it would be best if he remained silent on the subject.

******

Rahul Mehra had seen the newspaper. He had seen Paul's interview on TV. He recollected Justin telling him that American agencies were trying to gather some evidence. Had they got the evidence? Justin had urged him to go through his old emails to see if he had any evidence that could be used against Paul. He looked at the clock. It was almost lunchtime. As usual, he went to the kitchen to prepare his meal. While preparing lunch, it suddenly struck him that Lalit had handed him a pen drive, which he hadn't opened. Where was that pen drive? He had almost forgotten about it. True, this was ten years back. He tried to recollect where he could have kept that pen drive. Rahul Mehra, during his posting in NCB, had a unique habit. For all important cases, he would ask his staff to copy the details. He developed this habit for the simple reason that in case the manual file got misplaced, a soft copy would always be available. In such enforcement departments, there was always the possibility of manipulation by the staff in the lower rungs of the ladder. So, this was his safety measure.

Rahul's transfer from the NCB to the Indian High Commission at London was so sudden that he hadn't got the opportunity to collect his belongings from his office. But he remembered Lalit handing him the pen drive and that was perhaps two days prior to his second meeting with the

Chapter 31

minister. He would have to recollect those two days. He used to bring home the pen drives and label each of them, mentioning its contents. However, he hadn't even seen these pen drives.

Rahul finished his meal and lay down for a nap. After fifteen minutes, he got up. He felt restless and decided to search for the pen drive. It must be lying somewhere with him only. He started searching. In the upper shelf of the cupboard of his bedroom was a cardboard carton. He took it out and opened it. Yes, there were CDs and pen drives, numerous of them. He sat down and started examining the markings on them, one by one. On some of the pen drives, the markings had faded while on some others the sticker had torn off.

He distinctly remembered that the particular pen drive handed to him by Lalit wasn't marked. So, he started picking out all those pen drives which were unmarked or without a sticker. These were nine in number. He carried these to the living room and began the arduous task of checking the contents of each pen drive on his laptop.

******

Sanjeev, Shankar and Ayesha were sitting in Sheela's cabin. Ayesha excitedly narrated how she happened to meet Ashutosh and that she had got him to agree to signing a contract.

Looking pleased, Sheela said, 'So, he agreed, great. He must be happy. His book is going to be published by Spellers.'

'Yes, but he seemed a little apprehensive,' Ayesha said.

'Why?'

'I couldn't make that out ... I sensed it.'

Shankar said, 'Did you ask him who was responsible for the marketing and how it became a bestseller?'

'No, I was more interested in getting the publishing rights,' Ayesha replied.

Sheela grimaced, 'I've told all of you a number of times that our job is to publish. We are not to go into the background. What matters is that the author shouldn't have a criminal background and the contents of the book aren't offensive or violative of human values. That's all.'

'You're right, ma'am. The manuscript and the book have been read by Mr Anand Banerjee as well as by me. The contents are okay. Ashutosh's wife Sujata is my sister's friend. Both husband and wife are lecturers in Delhi University,' Ayesha elaborated.

'Why don't you call him here? We'd like to meet him,' Sheela suggested.

'Sure. I'm meeting him this evening and I'll tell him,' Ayesha said, and as they stood up to go back to their respective desks, she informed Sheela, 'I'll draft a contract and will get it signed by him today.'

'Go ahead, there's no problem.'

'But he may not be interested in getting it immediately published through us.'

'Why?' Sheela was surprised.

'I don't know ... it's a gut feeling I have. I'll talk to him about this today.'

Sanjeev said, 'We can defer the contract also.'

Sheela shook her head, 'Get the contract signed and convince him for immediate publishing.'

'I'll manage that,' Ayesha promised, as she pushed open the door and they went out of Sheela's cabin.

******

Ashutosh had called Ganesh Salakar and fixed up a meeting. Ganesh had asked him to come to the American library any time after 2 p.m.

Chapter 31

When Ashutosh reached the American library, it was about 3 p.m. He had been there once before, along with some classmates, when he was in college. He had also seen the British Council library. These libraries had a wide range of books.

Uncle met him at the gate and they went inside the library. They sat at a large table.

Ganesh affectionately patted Ashutosh's shoulder and said sadly, 'I've made things uncomfortable for you. I'm sorry. I should have told you earlier about the last chapter.'

Ashutosh remained silent. Ganesh continued in the same low tone, 'I felt extremely guilty that day. I've betrayed your trust; I know Sujata must be very annoyed with me.'

Ashutosh just looked at him mournfully and finally said, 'Uncle, why did you do that? We're a peace-loving couple. We don't want to become embroiled in any controversy.'

'I know. I had no idea of Olivia's intention. Had I known at that time, I wouldn't have inserted that last chapter. I wasn't aware of their intention. Please believe me, Ashutosh.'

'Uncle, the actual incident pertaining to a minister and chief of NCB is dangerous. Today, the chief has contacted us. Tomorrow, the minister may come to know.'

'Nothing of that sort will happen ... that I can assure you.'

'Uncle, I'm sorry, I cannot go by your assurances now,' Ashutosh said stiffly, and then in a voice that left no doubt how much he was still hurting, 'Spellers had sent an email. They were interested in publishing the book. You never told me.'

'Yes, I didn't tell you,' Ganesh sighed. 'The time wasn't right. They wanted to track the chief. They were in that process. The appearance of any publisher at that stage would have been improper.'

'Anyway, Spellers has approached me now … again. They want me to sign the contract.'

'You can do it. I'm sure there won't be any objection now.'

'Spellers had my original manuscript, which had thirty chapters. They're now asking me to forward a *complete* manuscript, one that has all thirty-one chapters.'

'Your book has become popular and it has thirty-one chapters and it has to be of thirty-one chapters now. It isn't advisable to change it.'

Ashutosh looked at Ganesh and said bluntly, 'Uncle, that's not the issue. They're professional. They may ask for reasons behind inserting the thirty-first chapter at a later stage. If they ask, which I'm sure they will, shall I tell them the real reason? Shall I tell them that it has *factual narration*? I'm getting associated with a top publisher, Uncle. I cannot hide anything from them!'

Ganesh wasn't in a position to reply. The publisher would ask in all likelihood and Ashutosh's assumption wasn't unfounded. Ganesh wasn't sure if Olivia or his senior would like to have it told.

He said softly, once again affectionately patting his protégé's back, 'Ashutosh, I love you. I've already annoyed you. If you don't mind, I can take Olivia's suggestion. She's sitting in her cabin … it'll take just a couple of minutes. Can you please wait for a few minutes?'

Ashutosh nodded. He was expecting this sort of response. Ganesh disappeared and was back within ten minutes. 'I've talked to Olivia. She says you can go ahead. You can tell them the reason if they ask. The real reason – that I told you the other day,' Ganesh sounded relieved.

'Thank you, Uncle. That has taken a huge burden off my mind. I feel lighter. I can talk or negotiate freely with them now.'

Chapter 31

'Ashutosh … may I give you a bit of personal advice …?' Ganesh hesitated.

'Yes?'

'If possible, sign the contract now but see if you can defer the printing for some time.'

'Why? I think that's not fair.'

'I don't have any reason. It's just an intuition. It's your decision.'

Ashutosh got up and slowly said, 'Uncle, you should leave this job. It's not meant for people like you.'

He left the building.

Chapter – 19

Justin Brown was sitting at the American Center in New Delhi. He had Rahul Mehra's email address. This was the email address through which he had sought a meeting with Ashutosh. Rahul had a Gmail account, and it was his private account. Justin wasn't sure how many years old this would be. He pondered for some time whether this very Gmail account existed ten years back. He made a call to his headquarters in Virginia. His colleague picked up the phone. They were talking on an unlisted number.

'Hello? Adam?' Justin said.

'Yes?' Adam Smith asked.

'Justin here.'

'Yes, Justin. How are you?'

'Fine.'

'Anything urgent? It's early morning here.'

'I know, I know. I need some information.'

'What's it about?'

'How old is Gmail?'

'What do you mean "how old"?'

'Just tell me, Adam – did Gmail exist about ten years back? Say, in 2008.'

'Yes, definitely. Gmail started on April Fool's Day – on 1 April 2004.'

'Okay, if I give you a Gmail address can you tell me when it was created?'

'You want to know whether the particular Gmail account was operative in 2008.'

'Yes. It's operative today. I need to know whether the person has been operating it since 2008.'

Chapter 31

'And your next question would be whether one can retrieve emails which are ten years old.'

'Yes.'

'And the question after that would be how can we retrieve those ten-year-old emails.'

Justin smiled and said, 'Please find out for me. It's rather urgent.'

'It may not be possible to retrieve old emails, Justin.'

'Please talk to a technical support person. I'm waiting.'

'I'll call back in half an hour,' and Adam disconnected.

Adam was a software professional and he could unlock any account, unless it had been protected with double security protection. In normal course, an email address is protected only by a password. Adam noted down Rahul's email address and started scanning through his desktop. It took him about twenty minutes. The said email account was opened sometime in 2006 and was operative since then. The number of emails wasn't much. In the last several years, the total number of emails received and sent was 334. That meant, on an average, only twenty-one emails per year had been sent and received. In fact, it had remained inoperative for about three years in between and scarcely operated over the last one year. Even now, it wasn't used frequently. Adam called Justin and apprised him of the details. Now Justin asked him to retrieve the old emails; he gave Adam a specific date in 2008 and told him that every single email from that date onwards would be required. Adam kept trying. Since the number of emails were not much, he could retrieve the emails of the last four years only and not prior to that.

Adam phoned Justin and said, 'I'm giving you a password, a new one that I've generated. You can use it and open the mailbox. You'll be able to see all the emails of the last three years.'

'Okay, but I'm interested in all emails since 2008. Find a way out. You must have done this earlier,' Justin kept up the pressure.

'I'll have to talk to someone in Google.'

'Why?'

'Gmail is a Google product, Justin.'

'Then talk to them.'

'It's not that easy, my friend; be warned. Google has strict by-laws of their own. Their employees cannot keep track of other people's emails.'

'But they must have the tools to open deleted emails?'

'Definitely. But we cannot compel them and ask them to go against their own by-laws. And you know they have a system, Justin. Whoever tries to open, can be tracked. They could lose their job and, not only that, their reputation will be so adversely impacted that they wouldn't get a job elsewhere ever again!'

'Just try. Please manage it, Adam. I know you can do it. It's crucial.'

'I'll see what can be done,' he promised.

Adam disconnected his phone, and looked at his watch; it was 8.30 a.m. The staff had started pouring in. Adam discussed the matter with the technical support team. They expressed their inability when they were told to retrieve deleted emails.

******

Justin scanned the emails of three years. Nothing of interest. These were all personal emails that Rahul had mostly sent to or received from his daughter or son-in-law. There was no email suggesting any drug case whatsoever. Some were promotional emails, bank statements or with credit card details. It was expected because Rahul was inactive for the last several years and, based on his own observation, Rahul

Chapter 31

preferred to stay in isolation. By the looks of it, he was an introvert. Justin looked at his watch and decided to call it a day. He was staying in a hotel because he was in India for a short mission and it was considered inadvisable to rent an apartment. He collected his things together, stuffed them into his office bag, called for a cab and left the American Center.

******

Ayesha was having dinner with Ashutosh and Sujata at their residence. She had brought along with her a copy of the contract for Ashutosh to sign. They were chatting like old friends over their meal, and the conversation eventually turned to Spellers.

'I was talking with Sheela Ma'am today and told her I had met you.'

'Did she agree to publish?' Ashutosh asked eagerly.

'Oh yes. Do you remember, I'd told you that she was trying to trace you? Our office had sent emails expressing our interest in publishing your book.'

'She seems to be a nice lady,' Sujata observed between mouthfuls.

Ayesha laughed heartily, 'Nooooo! The owners of top publishing houses are all eccentric. You should see their tantrums.'

'Really?' asked Sujata, surprised.

'Yes, really. Have you heard of Mr Srinivasan, the business tycoon?'

'Yes,' Ashutosh said, taking one more chapatti.

'His wife sent us a manuscript. It was a brilliant, well-researched and informative work. I have seen the script. I recommended it to Sheela Ma'am, that it would be a good one to have on our catalogue. She didn't pay any heed. One fine morning, Mrs Srinivasan came to meet her. She had taken an appointment but Sheela Ma'am made her sit at the reception for two hours!' Ayesha paused to drink some water.

'But why?' Sujata asked, puzzled.

'No particular reason. And it's not only Sheela Ma'am. It's with all established publishers. Just to show their value,' she shrugged her shoulders.

'Then did you publish her book?' asked Ashutosh.

'Yeah, after much persuasion by our VP and a number of calls from Mr Srinivasan.'

'Surprising. I thought they're all educated and decent people.'

'Educated, yes, but not decent.'

They finished their meal and Ayesha helped Sujata and Ashutosh in clearing the table. After a while, they were sitting in the living room. Ayesha booked a cab and they chatted awhile about the upcoming US elections and Ayesha then steered their conversation back to Spellers, regaling her hosts with a few anecdotes of some of their authors.

'Can you do one thing?' Ayesha addressed Ashutosh, after they had had a hearty laugh about the demands of a particularly famous author.

'What do you have in mind?'

'Please come to our office tomorrow – anytime that is convenient to you. Sheela Ma'am would like to meet you.'

'Is it a ritual?' Ashutosh chuckled.

'No, no,' Ayesha grinned. 'In fact, she prefers not to meet any author. She has never been interested. It's an exception in your case. She specifically asked me this.'

'I'll come. I'll be there, no problem.'

'What time will be convenient for you? I'll ensure that she's available.'

Ashutosh thought for a while, and then asked her, 'Say, around 12.30 p.m.? Will that be okay? My class ends at 12 noon tomorrow.'

Chapter 31

'That's perfect,' Ayesha said, pulling out an envelope from her shoulder bag, and then the contract from that envelope. She proffered it to Ashutosh, beaming.

'Please sign it.'

'Shall I do it now or tomorrow before Sheela?'

'This is part of our job ... She doesn't care about these routine matters. You may sign it now. Tomorrow's meeting is a mere formality.'

'Okay,' Ashutosh said and signed at the bottom of each page. The contract ran into six pages.

'I'll email it to you after I fill all the other details for your reference, okay?' Just then Ayesha's cab arrived, and after thanking them for an excellent dinner, she left.

******

Rahul scanned those nine pen drives one by one. One pen drive contained the addresses and contact numbers of his core team when he was the NCB chief. That was meant as a ready reference. The second pen drive had briefs of all the cases made during his tenure in NCB, except, of course, the last one. The third pen drive contained the resumes of each of the officers for recording their annual confidential reports. The fourth pen drive had some film songs of that period. The remaining five pen drives had data related to five different cases, copied from various documents.

Rahul carefully scrutinized each of these five pen drives but it seemed to him that none of these pertained to the case relating to Paul. Though he hadn't seen earlier as to what exactly was in the laptop, he still remembered that Lalit Gaur had specifically told him that the name 'Paul' had been referred to at a number of places. In none of these five pen drives was there any mention of 'Paul'. So, it was clear to him that these pen drives didn't have the data relating to the last case. He kept aside all these pen drives and pasted a sticker on each one of them.

That done, he leant forward on his desk, chin resting on one palm, eyes closed, going back in time, to that day, ten years ago. He desperately tried to recollect where he had kept the pen drive when Lalit had handed it over to him. He wouldn't have kept it in his cabin. It was the same day the minister had ordered him to release the five accused people. It was the most shocking day of his life. He had been confused. He had felt belittled in front of his subordinate staff. Could it be that he had left the pen drive on his desk, or in the drawer, in that agitated state of mind? But then, he had gone to that office, that cabin and had sat at the same desk for another two days. Had it been left there he would have noticed it. He was assuring himself that the pen drive wasn't left in the office. If that be the case, then the pen drive must be somewhere in his home.

He decided to make one last attempt to find the missing pen drive.

Chapter – 20

Aneesh had taken a cab, instead of his official car. Last night he had received a message from Peter Avilov that he was staying at the Hyatt in New Delhi. Peter had come for a day. He sent a message to Aneesh requesting an urgent meeting with him. The cab entered the Hyatt premises. Aneesh got down from the cab and entered the lobby to find Peter waiting for him. They sat in the lobby itself.

'How come you're here?' Aneesh asked.

'A delegation was coming to attend a three-day film festival, which is to start from today, somewhere near Mandi House. I came along with them. But I've to leave tonight,' Peter sounded tired.

'What's the urgency?' Aneesh asked without beating around the bush.

'Have you got any information on Rahul Mehra?'

'Not yet. I hope to get the details by today, end of day. I've spoken with our Home Department. The state police are on the job. But why are you so concerned?'

'I told you the other day that this person might have some information on Paul Johnson, which may jeopardize Paul's chances of winning the election.'

'But, according to you, they have initiated an adverse campaign against Paul even in the absence of any evidence,' Aneesh pointed out.

'That's a name-smearing campaign,' Peter said a trifle impatiently. 'In your country also, when elections are held, candidates go on making allegations against opponents and then keep on apologizing. I see that as a first step towards some major controversy.'

'You're not sure whether Rahul has any evidence or not. Maybe he doesn't even remember that case?'

'It's possible,' Peter admitted reluctantly. 'But that's exactly what we want to know ... why are the American agencies after him.'

'Last time you told me that your intelligence had intercepted some messages that Rahul has been contacted by an American agent – have they got any more information?'

'The only information is that the agent and Rahul haven't contacted each other after one meeting.'

'Are you sure?'

'That's what our intelligence says.'

'Then there is a possibility that Rahul has nothing in his possession.'

'We're also assuming the same. But that's an assumption. We want to be sure.'

'I think I'll get some information on Rahul Mehra by this evening.'

'There's one more thing. Since Paul has dissociated himself from all past drug-related contacts, all his present associates, colleagues, friends and family are not aware of his involvement in narcos. After that statement by Sarah Baker, he must be getting desperate to take help of some old associate, but that's risky. I'm sure Steve has him under surveillance. One wrong move on Paul's part and Steve will put him in a soup.'

'That's not our problem,' Aneesh said firmly.

'What we want is that Paul has to be cautioned about this.'

Aneesh couldn't follow the direction of Peter's statement. 'Why are you telling me this?' he asked.

Peter let out a long deep breath and then asked, looking at Aneesh directly, 'Can you help us in this regard? Any move on our part will get noticed.'

Chapter 31

Taken aback, Aneesh said, 'I'm sorry, Peter. I've already told you that we don't want to embroil ourselves in all this. If Russians will get noticed, Indians too will get noticed. You have to handle that yourself. You have so many friendly countries. Take their help.'

'India is negotiating a deal with Russia for getting anti-aircraft equipment, S-400. You're aware of this, surely.' Peter tried another approach.

'Yes, I'm aware of it. In fact, I'm part of the negotiating team.'

'I can help in finalizing the deal.'

'Look, Peter. Don't make any such move,' Aneesh advised. 'You're a diplomat. You can very well understand a diplomat's position. He has to be a hard negotiator but he's also expected to strike a balance.'

'So, you refuse?' Peter's tone expressed his displeasure.

'As far as Rahul Mehra is concerned, I've promised you, we'll definitely cooperate. But the second proposal is dangerous.'

'You don't need to give a final reply in the negative right now. You take your time,' Peter advised him smilingly. 'You may discuss at your end.'

'Okay. Is that all?' Aneesh said while getting up.

'Yes. Please let me know as soon as you get anything on Rahul Mehra.'

'Sure,' Aneesh assured him as they shook hands, their meeting coming to an end.

Aneesh requested the hotel staff to arrange a cab for him.

******

When he entered Spellers, Ayesha was already at the reception, waiting for him. They shook hands and Ayesha escorted Ashutosh to Sheela Nair's cabin.

'Ma'am, Mr Ashutosh,' Ayesha said, introducing him.

'Good afternoon,' Ashutosh said politely.

'Good afternoon,' Sheela reciprocated with a smile.

'Ma'am, I met him yesterday and he has signed the contract for the publishing rights of *The Grass*,' Ayesha updated her.

Sheela smiled at Ashutosh, as they all sat down. She looked at him, trying to assess him. A young man in his early thirties, a lecturer of English literature. He was wearing brown trousers and an orange shirt. A studious-looking man.

'You've become famous worldwide at such a young age,' Sheela said warmly.

Ashutosh lowered his head, acknowledging her compliment, but said nothing.

'Do you know, when I came to know that a novel by an Indian author has made it to the top ten bestsellers, I grew interested, Ayesha must have told you.'

'Yes, ma'am,' Ashutosh said.

'You're so modest. You didn't get your photograph printed on your book.'

Ashutosh kept quiet.

'You're such a smart, handsome man. You should get your photograph on the back cover, like any other author,' Sheela continued, charmingly.

Ayesha noticed Sheela was praising Ashutosh, which was rare. Sheela Nair was not in the habit of appreciating anyone other than her own self.

'How did you achieve that?' Sheela asked.

'Achieve what, ma'am?'

'How did you manage to reach the bestseller slot? Look, I'm a businesswoman. I'm interested only in selling. To look at the contents of a book isn't my prerogative. Ayesha looks after all that.'

Chapter 31

'I've simply written the book. One of my college professors helped me in editing and marketing this book. He has always been very fond of me and I've the highest regard for him. Over the years, I started looking upon him as my uncle. He has retired now,' Ashutosh explained.

'That's fascinating. I'd like to meet your uncle one day, Ashutosh. He has great marketing skills.' Sheela looked at Ayesha and said, 'Can you please arrange for some coffee?'

'Sure,' Ayesha said and left, returning within a few minutes, carrying a tray with three cups of coffee.

All three of them settled down with their respective coffee cup.

Sheela said, 'We have a literary agent. He has seen your book and he observed that the last chapter in your book is, well, a sort of misfit. He was, of course, looking at it from a literary angle. Ayesha, who is our chief editor, too was of the same opinion. What made you add the last chapter?'

'Yes, please tell us because your original manuscript had thirty chapters and speaking from our experience, the novel was complete in all respect at Chapter 30,' Ayesha chipped in eagerly.

Ashutosh looked at both of them and said, 'Yes, I'll tell you. It has an interesting background. Perhaps "interesting" may not be the correct word. In fact, I've come here to meet you as well as to tell you about this background. I know there is a probability that you may decide against publishing my book after hearing me out, but I feel I must tell you.'

Both ladies grew curious and looked at each other. Sheela said, 'Please go on.'

Ashutosh began by telling them why the manuscript was given to his uncle, Ganesh Salakar, and that it was he who had inserted Chapter 31. The book was subsequently printed, that Ganesh took over the promotion and marketing aspects and that Ashutosh and Sujata were ecstatic at the rising popularity of the novel. Then he told them about his meeting with Rahul Mehra and it was the first time that he, Ashutosh, came to know that the events of the last chapter weren't fictitious but bore close similarity with some true facts. He later confronted Ganesh on this – the same uncle, for whom he had great regard. It was only then that Ganesh revealed to him that it was a ploy to reach Rahul Mehra, who was an ex-chief of the NCB. He told both the ladies that Ganesh was aware of the ploy but he hadn't told them until they confronted him. That came as a shock to both Ashutosh and Sujata. He also told them that after meeting Ayesha, he had met Ganesh and told him that there was an offer from Spellers and that Ashutosh wanted to tell the background to Spellers before they went ahead with the printing.

When he finished, Sheela asked, 'Why didn't you tell Ayesha at the first meeting?'

'I wanted to inform my uncle before telling you. When she told me that I must meet you, I thought it better to tell it directly to you. I didn't want to spoil the relationship between my publisher and me, as the author, by hiding something. Now I feel that it was a blunder to add Chapter 31. It wasn't necessary. It's a complete misfit.'

Ayesha was taken by surprise on hearing Ashutosh's recounting of events. She recollected that Ashutosh had been somewhat hesitant when she had first met him at his residence.

Sheela had a grave expression as she reflected on what Ashutosh had just revealed. She wasn't bothered that the last chapter wasn't fictitious. Nor was she worried that it was a misfit. But she was definitely concerned that it was inserted in the book with a specific purpose and that too without the knowledge of the author. It was for her to take the decision. She looked straight at Ashutosh and made an attempt to smile as she addressed him.

'Thank you, Ashutosh. I'm glad you were honest with us … you could have chosen to remain silent. I appreciate your courage. Don't worry about the publishing part. We'll go ahead.'

Chapter 31

Ashutosh was now free from any sort of guilt. He thanked the ladies for their cooperation and stood up to leave, and came out of Sheela's cabin, relieved and happy.

Sheela spoke to Ayesha, 'Don't talk about this with anybody. It should remain between us.'

'I understand, ma'am,' Ayesha said.

'And defer the printing. I'll let you know when to go for it.'

'Yes, ma'am.'

'You needn't tell Ashutosh about the deferment.'

'Ashutosh is yet to forward the full manuscript of thirty-one chapters. I'll not insist on that and it would get automatically delayed on that account.'

When Ayesha was back in her cabin, Sanjeev and Shankar came to her, eager to know what was going on.

'Was that Ashutosh with you and ma'am?' Sanjeev demanded.

'Yeah, Sheela Ma'am wanted to meet him once, before we start publishing his book.'

'Strange, she hardly meets any author,' Sanjeev looked at Ayesha trying to learn something from her expression.

'Yeah, I know, but she asked me to call him,' Ayesha's face and tone were both expressionless.

Shankar said unhappily, 'You could have introduced him to us. You know how desperately I'd been looking for him and, finally, when he was here, he left without meeting us.'

'I'm sorry but Ashutosh was in a hurry. I'll ask him for lunch someday, you can meet him then.'

Shankar could see that Ayesha wasn't looking as excited as she had been the other day, and wondered why. He wasn't aware of the way the meeting had ended.

Chapter – 21

Rahul brought a stool and placed it near the opened cupboard. He climbed on to it to have a look at the upper shelf of the cupboard, where he had kept the carton. There was a possibility that the pen drive he was looking for may have fallen outside the carton somehow. No, it wasn't there. He lifted some old shirts lying on the shelf to look beneath them. It wasn't there. He stepped down from the stool and went to his writing table, and opened its two drawers which were filled with miscellaneous articles. He took out both the drawers and emptied these on the floor. There wasn't a single pen drive. He was hoping to find it there. Feeling a bit disappointed, Rahul cursed himself for not keeping things in an organized manner. A pen drive was such a small thing that it could be anywhere. He spent two hours looking for it. Finally, he called his daughter in the US.

'Hello, beta.'

'Hello, Papa,' his daughter greeted him over the phone.

'How are you, beta? How's everything?'

'We're fine, Papa. How are you? You haven't called since you returned,' she complained.

'I did call when I landed in Delhi,' he reminded her.

'Oh, that,' her tone was dismissive. 'That was just an "arrival call".'

Rahul laughed.

'Are you taking your meals properly?' she asked him affectionately.

'Yes, yes. You know I'm fond of cooking. Don't worry, beta.'

Chapter 31

'And how's the weather?'

'Summer's here, so ... Just tell me one thing, beta. I was looking for some old pen drives. Do you remember where these could be?'

'Yes. These were in a cardboard carton in your cupboard. I had collected all the CDs and pen drives and put them there.'

'I found that carton but I was looking for a particular pen drive and I can't find it. Could there be any other place that I should look at?'

'Is it an old one?'

'Yeah, maybe about ten years old.'

She pondered for a while and then said, 'Then it must be in that carton only, Papa. Try once again. I'm sure it's there.'

'Okay, I'll look again.'

'Okay, bye, Papa, take care, love you!'

'Love you, too, beta, bye,' Rahul disconnected the line.

He again emptied the carton. All the pen drives were distinctly marked and he looked at those markings. He thought of checking the contents of every single pen drive just to reassure himself that the pen drive he was looking for wasn't among these.

******

Sheela was strongly tempted to share the background of Chapter 31 with Anand. He was the closest friend she had. She had always confided in him whenever she wanted to share or discuss something. In fact, she had even confided in Anand her marital problems. But a niggling doubt forced her to reconsider. Would it be appropriate to tell Anand that the last chapter of *The Grass* was actually meant for tracking the ex-chief of NCB and that too by the Americans, she thought. She weighed the pros and cons in her mind, her brows furrowed.

Anand was good for discussing publishing matters. He was good for parties; and yes, he was good for flirting, but was he matured enough to understand the implications in this case? No, perhaps not. She decided against it. She shouldn't share such vital and delicate information with Anand.

But she needed to talk to someone. But who? She thought of Aneesh. Yes, he's mature, he's intelligent, she thought. Aneesh had shown his eagerness and desire to meet her when they had last met at the airport before their flight to Hyderabad. She somehow still liked Aneesh. She picked up her mobile phone and called him. Aneesh didn't pick up; she disconnected. After a while her phone rang; it was Aneesh.

'Hello?' came Aneesh's voice from the other end.

'Hello, Sheela this side.'

'You don't have to tell me. I know your number; I know your voice.' Sheela could feel the smile in his voice.

'That's nice to hear. Are you busy?'

'A little bit.'

'Can we meet this evening?'

Aneesh realized that it would be perhaps more than a year since Sheela had last called.

'We can keep it at night.'

'Night?' Sheela hesitated.

'What's so strange? We've spent a number of nights together.'

'Okay, we can have dinner together but forget about spending the night.'

'My place or yours?'

'I'm inviting. Come over to my place,' Sheela said in a crisp voice.

'Okay. I'll be there, at about nine,' Aneesh confirmed, and they disconnected.

Chapter 31

It was then that Sheela saw there was a missed call from Anand – he had called her when she was talking to Aneesh. That day, after so many years, she decided not to call back.

******

It was 4 p.m. Justin had so far not received any information from Adam Smith, his colleague in Virginia. He had sent a reminder in the morning.

Even if one has the password, one cannot retrieve such old emails as these get automatically deleted. Steve had also not asked him to do any specific work other than keep a watch on Rahul. He picked up his phone and again called Adam.

'Hello?' Justin said.

'I'm on your job. Don't worry. The boys in the technical support team are hopeful,' Adam said as soon as he heard his voice.

'That's good to hear.'

'As soon as I get some information, I'll forward it to you.'

'Thanks, Adam.'

The line went dead.

******

The doorbell rang. Sujata opened the door to see Ayesha at their doorstep. 'Hello,' grinned Sujata warmly.

'I'm sorry, I came unannounced.'

'Oh, no need to apologize! You're always welcome.' Sujata held the door wide open, for Ayesha to come inside.

'Is Ashutosh at home?' Ayesha asked, still standing outside.

'Yes, yes. Please come in,' assured Sujata.

Ayesha smiled her thanks and they sat down in the living room.

Ashutosh had heard the doorbell. He too came into the living room. He saw Ayesha and smiled, 'At this hour?' Ashutosh asked. 'All okay?'

'I wanted to talk to you after all that you said at the office this morning.'

'It was necessary,' he replied, sitting down on a single sofa opposite them. 'I didn't want to hide anything.'

Sujata said, 'Yes. We thought everything should be clearly informed to Sheela Nair.'

'Are you aware of the reason behind the insertion of Chapter 31?' Ayesha asked Sujata.

'Yes, I was with Ashutosh when we confronted Uncle Ganesh.'

'You did the right thing. Had it been known at a later date, my position would have been embarrassing,' Ayesha told them both.

'I wanted to tell you at the first meeting itself but then I thought it should be brought to the knowledge of your Sheela Ma'am directly,' Ashutosh explained.

'That was a wise decision, thank you.'

'What was her reaction?' Sujata asked her curiously.

Ayesha kept quiet for a while and then decided to be forthright with them. 'After you left, she told me not to share the information with any of my colleagues and she also asked me to defer the printing of the book. I think she will need some time to make up her mind.'

'That's not a problem. It's fine with me,' Ashutosh said reassuringly.

'Sujata, your husband is a very good and honest man,' Ayesha exclaimed. 'What he said today needs a lot of courage.'

'Don't pamper him!' Sujata laughed.

'So, I'm not to send you the complete manuscript right now?' Ashutosh asked.

Chapter 31

'I'll tell you when to send it. I'll follow-up with Sheela.'

'Thank you, Ayesha, for all the interest you're taking in this book.'

'Oh, please, it's nothing! Please don't be so formal,' Ayesha gently brushed aside Ashutosh's words of gratitude. 'I'm very curious about one thing: tell me, you must have felt bad when Ganesh Salakar told you everything?'

'Bad?' Sujata rolled her eyes, 'We felt we had been cheated, misused!'

'Do you feel whatever Mr Salakar told you would be the exact intention or could there be something beyond that?'

'I think whatever uncle told us would obviously be whatever was told to him. I'm sure he's not hiding anything more now. If there's actually something larger than that, then definitely uncle has no knowledge of it,' Ashutosh said firmly.

'But why are you asking this?'

'Just out of curiosity, Sujata, nothing else,' Ayesha shrugged.

Ashutosh looked at Ayesha intently and asked, 'Sheela had asked you not to share this with anyone. Is there any guarantee that she herself will not discuss this with anyone?'

'I think she won't, Ashutosh. She is pretty matured. Though there is one person she might confide in – Anand Banerjee.'

'Who is he?'

'He's a literary agent associated with Spellers but he's close to Sheela.'

'How close?' Sujata asked, smiling.

'Very close,' Ayesha grinned. 'Still, I'm sure Sheela is intelligent enough not to confide in him regarding this matter.'

Sujata asked Ayesha to have dinner with them as it was dinner time but Ayesha excused herself and left their place.

Chapter – 22

One full day had passed. Justin was expecting some information from Adam any moment. At night, after having dinner at one of the hotel's in-house restaurants, he was back in his room. He heard a notification on his phone. It was from Adam. He immediately opened his email on his phone. Adam had forwarded a link. He opened his laptop, opened his email and clicked on the link. The details of all 334 emails of Rahul Mehra, whether sent or received, were there. Wonderful, he thought. He started scanning the emails from 2008 onwards; emails from November 2008 could be of importance. There were thirty received emails and ten sent emails. From December 2008 onwards, the number of emails received had reduced to almost nil. Justin concentrated on those forty emails of November 2008. That was perhaps the period when the case was being prepared and Rahul was asked to release the detainees. While reading the emails, Justin realized that the majority of the sent emails comprised Rahul's letters to his daughter, and from the contents he gathered that Rahul's daughter was settled in the US. These were the usual family emails.

Then he started checking the received emails. Most of these were from his daughter. Justin had forgotten that it was Rahul's personal email address. There was hardly any possibility of official communication on this email address. However, he kept looking. Then, he saw there was an email sent by one Malini; it had been sent in November 2008. That was the last email received in that month and what was interesting was that it hadn't been opened. Justin opened it. A folder was attached with the email. He downloaded it and opened the folder. There was a collection of documents. This seemed to be the details of some drug case. The first

Chapter 31

document was the seizure memo. And four statements. He started reading the statements. It took him hardly any time to deduce that all these documents were related to Paul Johnson's case.

Justin was excited and thrilled. He had hit the bullseye, finally! This was exactly what he had been hoping for, looking for. The seizure memo narrated the procedure of how heroin had been seized in the presence of two independent witnesses. There wasn't any mention of Paul's name. The statement of three people who were to receive the drugs were also usual statements but without any reference to Paul. It was the fourth statement, that of Ajeet Singh, which was significant. Exhilarated, Justin got up, poured some wine in a glass and returned to his laptop. Ajeet Singh's statement ran into seven pages. The initial two paragraphs were routine. Then it went on to say,

> *I admit that I had come to the aforesaid address to deliver 30kg of heroin along with one accomplice. This was given to me by Yunus, who lives in Bombay. Yunus works for Samuel Garcia. I've never met Samuel Garcia but I've heard Yunus referring to Samuel's name repeatedly.*

The statement went on, wherein Ajeet Singh narrated as to how he was introduced to drug trading. He had admitted that he was a carrier and used to deliver drugs throughout India as per Yunus's directions. Thereafter, it appeared that he was shown the contents of one of the laptops. He went on to say,

> *Today two laptops were taken from the car in which we had come to make a delivery. I was asked to unlock the laptop by giving the password. I didn't remember the password of one of the laptops. I was asked to try to open it by making various combinations of alphabets and numerals but I wasn't successful. The officers also tried by putting in different passwords by way of hit and trial but we weren't able to unlock it. Regarding the second laptop, I gave the password, as I was aware of the same. It*

was opened by the officer with my consent in my presence and in presence of two witnesses. The officer continued looking at the contents. They could open the mailbox as well as one of the folders.

Justin thought that Rahul was wrong when he told him that the laptops couldn't be opened. Here was the evidence that one of the two laptops was unlocked. The contents were seen and confirmed by Ajeet Singh. Ajeet Singh had further stated,

I was shown some of the emails, which were sent by Yunus to me and he had also forwarded some of the trail mails, which were sent by Samuel Garcia to Yunus. I was shown a specific email sent on 10th November by Samuel Garcia, wherein there is a reference to one Paul. On query as to who is this Paul, I hereby state that he was the man in America, and we've been told in the post that Paul is the main supplier of drugs from Columbia. On query, I state that I've only heard about Paul. I've never met Samuel or Paul. My only contact is with Yunus.

Ajeet Singh's statement continued. He was shown the contents of one of the folders. This folder comprised the names, addresses and contact numbers of various persons in India as well as in other countries. He stated,

The folder was opened and I was asked to explain the details. I've carefully seen the contents of the folder. It reflects the names, addresses, contact numbers of the persons to whom drugs are delivered. These persons are not the consumers but they further supply the drugs in respective cities as per the area earmarked to them. Some of these names are in codes. I'm not in a position to decipher the codes right now. In short, this folder has the complete distribution network.

The statement ended abruptly. It was apparently obtained hurriedly. Justin poured himself another drink

Chapter 31

and pondered over Ajeet Singh's statement. The laptops were returned. This was what was told by the cook and that was exactly what was ordered to Rahul. What astonished Justin was that Rahul hadn't opened this particular email. This meant that he was unaware of the existence of these documents. This email was sent to him at the end of November 2008. This was perhaps the only and the last email, which was official.

Justin resumed examining the received emails; there were very few emails. None from his office; none referring to the said case from any of his friends or colleagues. Ajeet Singh's statement had reference to 'Paul' but not 'Paul Johnson' and moreover it was the statement given by someone who might matter, or who might not. However, it definitely proved one thing: there was strong evidence in the shape of those laptops against Paul Johnson, but unfortunately the laptops had been returned. He eventually concluded it was up to Steve to decide whether these documents were useful, with special mention of the email sent by one Malini. That would be of interest to Steve.

******

Aneesh left his office a bit later than usual. He was somewhat dissatisfied that the local police had failed to find any information on Rahul Mehra. Aneesh was almost certain that either the Russian intelligence agencies had wrongly marked the name of Rahul Mehra or that Rahul Mehra was a deliberately created name used as a code in place of some other name. Aneesh's main concern was to know whether the person said to be Rahul Mehra actually had some knowledge about Paul Johnson and if so, how much would be its impact. Could that knowledge or document or whatever it was really change the course of the US presidential elections? Aneesh had never trusted the Russians.

Aneesh drove himself to Sheela's residence. Sheela had invited him for dinner. He didn't even remember when he had last visited Sheela's place.

There was a lot of traffic on the road. He looked at his watch and calculated that it would take him another twenty minutes to reach her house. Sheela had a big house in South Delhi, whereas Aneesh lived in a government accommodation in central Delhi. As usual, the locations of government accommodations were at the best of places but the accommodation in itself was not luxurious. These houses were moderately furnished.

It was ten minutes past nine when he parked his car outside Sheela's residence.

An elderly lady opened the door when he rang the doorbell. She exclaimed, 'Oh, good evening, sir, how lovely to see you!'

'Hello, Amma,' Aneesh grinned at her cheerfully. 'How have you been?'

'I'm fine, sir.'

Amma closed the door behind him, smiling contentedly. She had been working with Sheela for several years now. Aneesh didn't know her actual name but everyone called her Amma. Sheela was standing at the other end of the room. She came forward, hugged him and they settled down.

'How come a beautiful lady like you thought of inviting a person like me?' Aneesh teased.

'You're looking handsome,' Sheela said approvingly.

Aneesh laughed and said, 'You're joking! A man is either a bureaucrat or he's handsome.'

Amma came in holding a tray with a glass of water. She offered it to Aneesh.

'Ma'am told me that you're coming tonight for dinner. So, I prepared all the dishes myself,' she informed him, beaming from ear to ear.

Chapter 31

'Thank you, Amma,' Aneesh said simply, but his face expressed his pleasure at being there.

'You've come after a long time.'

'Your ma'am never called me before,' Aneesh said in a mock-complain tone.

'You needn't be invited. It's your house.' Amma protested stoutly.

'Of course! How is your daughter, Amma?'

'She's fine,' she gave him a toothy smile.

'Have you got her married?'

'I'm looking for a match, sir.'

'If you need any help at the time of marriage, you can always ask your ma'am. She's generous,' Aneesh winked at Sheela wickedly.

'I know, sir.'

Sheela, who had been quietly enjoying this banter between Aneesh and Amma, laughed and said, 'Aneesh too is generous.'

Amma smiled and left the room. Sheela got up and walked towards a counter where some bottles of wine were kept.

'What would you like to have?' she asked, turning around to face him.

'I'm not a habitual drinker.'

'What – would – you – like – to – have?' Sheela repeated, ignoring his statement.

'Give me any wine, the one you prefer for yourself.'

Sheela poured two drinks and came back to where they were sitting. They picked up their respective glasses, clinked the glasses and took a sip. Amma brought two plates, one with cheeseballs and the other with roasted kebabs. Sheela's phone rang. It was Anand; she declined the call.

Aneesh noted, without appearing to do so in an obvious way. He was aware of her friendship with Anand. He asked, 'Why didn't you answer his call?'

'It can wait. Let's enjoy our dinner tonight,' she said as she picked up the plate with the cheeseballs. She offered it to Aneesh. 'Amma makes awesome cheeseballs.'

'Yes, that she does!' said Aneesh biting into one.

Sheela wondered how she could bring up the topic. She waited till they finished their first drink. She got up and poured another one. As Aneesh took a sip, Sheela asked, 'Have you read *The Grass?*'

'What's it about?'

'It's a novel, written by an Indian author – you were holding it at the airport the other day, when we were both flying to Hyderabad.'

'Maybe, what's this about?' asked Aneesh, wondering what she had in mind.

'I met the author today in my office.'

'Okay, and ...?'

'I would like to tell you something about the book and the author.'

'Is it your publication?'

'No.'

'I may not be much interested,' warned Aneesh.

'I want to share it with you,' Sheela set down her half-empty wine glass.

'Okay, go ahead, I'm listening,' Aneesh said and picked up another cheeseball, holding the wine glass in the other hand.

Sheela started telling him about the book. Particularly the last chapter, the inclusion of which from the literary perspective didn't make any sense at all, and she narrated to him all that Ashutosh had told her and Ayesha at office.

Chapter 31

That the last chapter wasn't fictitious and that it had been inserted with the hope that perhaps the ex-chief of NCB would read it and contact the author. By this time, Aneesh had finished his second glass of wine. He himself went to the drinks' counter and poured out a third one for himself. He was getting curious and was thinking this was turning out to be a coincidence.

When Sheela finished, Aneesh asked, 'Do you have the book?'

'Yes. It may be in my car.'

'Can you get it, please? I'd like to see it.'

'Sure.' She got up, went out and returned with the book.

Aneesh turned to the last chapter and started reading it. It took him about fifteen minutes to complete it. He again read it and kept the book aside. Turning to face Sheela, he asked, 'So, you met this author Ashutosh today?'

'Yes. We'd shown interest in publishing the book but Ashutosh insisted that we should listen to the background first.'

'He himself volunteered to share the information?'

'Yes,' Sheela nodded, sipping from her glass.

'Did he tell you that he had met this ex-chief of NCB?'

'Yes. But when that ex-chief asked him as to how he had conceived the last chapter, he told him that it was his uncle who asked him to insert this chapter.'

'What is his name?' Aneesh tried to sound casual.

'Whose, the ex-chief or the uncle?'

'The ex-chief.'

'Rahul Mehra.'

'And who is this uncle?' Aneesh's mind was now racing.

'Ayesha told me that he was a professor in Delhi University and since his retirement he's been working with the American library.'

Aneesh finished his third drink. Sheela was looking at him, observing him carefully; Aneesh wasn't used to drinking. Sheela called Amma and asked her to serve dinner. Aneesh's thoughts were in a whirl: how did the Americans contact Rahul Mehra? He asked Sheela, 'How many of you know about these details?'

'Ayesha and me – why, Aneesh, what's happened?'

'Who is Ayesha?' Aneesh ignored her question.

'She's our chief editor. She brought Ashutosh and introduced me to him.'

'Have you shared this with Anand?'

'No. Why would I?' Sheela was getting irritated now with so many questions.

'Because he's close to you,' Aneesh replied promptly.

'Don't talk nonsense, Aneesh,' Sheela's voice arose by a notch or two.

'Tell me if I'm wrong,' he challenged her, suddenly sounding aggressive. 'You two are seen together in social circles ... you go to his place ... he comes to yours.'

'What's happened to you, Aneesh?' The alarm in Sheela's voice was palpable.

Aneesh sighed. He was quiet for a long time, flexing his shoulder and back muscles. He suddenly felt tired.

'Sheela,' Aneesh took a deep breath, 'this is something serious. Thank God you told me.'

'What's all this? Tell me,' Sheela demanded.

'No, let's have dinner first.'

'Aneesh–' Sheela pleaded.

'After dinner, Sheela,' came his terse reply.

Both of them sat down at the dining table. Sheela asked Amma to go to her room and rest.

Once Amma had gone out of earshot, they resumed their conversation over dinner.

Chapter 31

'Are you sure, you haven't shared with Anand?' Aneesh persisted.

'Why are you bringing him again in the conversation? Why don't you believe me, Aneesh?' Sheela was really cross now. 'I called you because I thought it's something to be shared with you. I haven't spoken about this with Anand. In fact, I haven't taken his calls the whole day.'

Aneesh silently looked at Sheela and started eating. He asked Sheela, 'Can you get me one last drink, please?'

'Are you sure? You're not used to much drinking.'

'I'm sure. Please get me a last one.'

Sheela brought some more wine and sat down with Aneesh. She gently placed her hand on Aneesh's arm and said, 'Will you please tell me something? What has happened that's so serious?'

'I can't tell you right now, Sheela. But yes, I'm thankful you called me and told me. It's extremely important.'

'Don't you trust me?' Sheela lay down her spoon and looked at him.

'I trust you, dear.'

'Then tell me – and believe me. I can keep it to myself.' Sheela resumed with her dinner.

'Yes, I know.'

'Please tell me. The suspense is too much, Aneesh! You've got me all curious now.'

'Okay. Listen carefully.'

Aneesh told her that American intelligence had been on the lookout for Rahul Mehra because they felt he might be in possession of some evidence. That the intelligence chief in the US wanted to use that evidence to damage the prospects of Paul Johnson winning the presidential election in the USA. The implications were far-reaching.

'We had the input but we weren't able to locate the whereabouts of Rahul Mehra. We knew he was living somewhere in Delhi but unfortunately our local police were unable to trace him,' Aneesh paused briefly and then asked her, 'Do you by any chance have his contact details?'

'Yes, he had met Ashutosh. I can get you Rahul's contact details. Ashutosh will definitely have it.'

'Can you get those details now?'

'Now?' Sheela said, taken aback.

'Yes,' Aneesh nodded gravely. 'It's only 11 p.m., Sheela.'

'But this isn't the time to call anyone. I'll get you the details tomorrow morning.'

Sheela realized that Aneesh was drunk. She served him some more rice. Aneesh looked at her adoringly, and lightly touched her cheeks.

'You're lovely, Sheela.'

'Finish your dinner and you can stay here for the night. I don't want you to drive now.'

'You're asking me to spend the night with you?' Aneesh couldn't believe he had heard right.

'It won't be the first time ... we've spent a number of nights together,' she said, laughing, and patted his shoulders.

'Okay, but you've promised you'll get me Rahul Mehra's contact details tomorrow morning.'

'Yes, yes, you selfish man!'

They laughed. Sheela thought it was after a long time that she had enjoyed dinner. Aneesh's company always gave her a feeling of security and confidence. Aneesh finished his dinner, burped and said to himself, so, Rahul Mehra does exist.

Chapter – 23

When he opened his eyes the next morning, he saw Sheela sleeping beside him. He looked at her; she was looking innocent. He leant towards her and kissed her cheek. Aneesh got up, opened the door and called out to Amma.

'Amma, can I get some tea?'

Hearing his voice, Sheela too woke up and requested Aneesh, 'Ask Amma to bring tea for me too.'

'I'm bringing it, sir,' Amma replied.

Aneesh sat down on the bed, yawning.

'What's the time?' Sheela asked.

'It's 7.30.'

'Did you sleep well?'

'Yes, like the good old days,' Aneesh smiled at her.

'Sir, what will you have for breakfast?' Amma asked as she brought in a tray with two cups of tea on it.

'Nothing for me, Amma, I'll be leaving soon.'

Sheela looked at Amma and said, 'He'll have breakfast here. Please prepare anything that he likes.'

As Amma left, Aneesh picked up his cup of tea, and asked softly, 'Sheela, have you ever wondered why we separated?'

Sheela didn't answer. She had no answer. She had asked this question umpteen number of times to herself, but had never found the answer. She simply said, 'Why don't you get ready and in the meantime I'll get you Rahul Mehra's contact details?'

'Sure,' Aneesh nodded.

In another half an hour, he was having breakfast. Amma had prepared grilled sandwiches and cutlets. Sheela was still in her nightdress. She came into the dining room and handed Aneesh a sheet of paper which had Rahul's telephone number and his email address.

Looking at it, he asked, 'Did you call Ashutosh?'

'No, I called Ayesha. She got it from Ashutosh.'

'Nice! Thank you, Sheela. You've done me a great favour.'

'Sometimes, you get too formal,' she gently brushed aside his thanks.

'I have to be. I'm a diplomat,' pat came his reply.

Sheela was about to say something but then stopped herself, shaking her head, smiling at Aneesh's enquiring look.

Aneesh finished breakfast and left Sheela's residence. While driving, Aneesh's thoughts went back to what Peter had been insisting all along; Peter had got the correct message. There *was* an NCB ex-chief, Rahul Mehra, staying in Delhi itself. He couldn't help but wonder how was it that there wasn't any record of him in the pension office. He had to call Peter but then decided that he would first talk with Rahul.

******

Rahul was fed up. He had tried to find the pen drive at almost all the possible places in his home. But there wasn't any pen drive anywhere except in that cardboard carton. He had examined each of those but he couldn't find the one relating to Paul Johnson's case. More than a month had passed, and there hadn't been any further communication from Justin Brown, the American, who had met him. Rahul was certain that Justin would be trying other sources to find some information that could be used as evidence against

Chapter 31

Paul. In fact, ever since he had met Justin, Rahul had been following the news pertaining to the US presidential election with far greater interest than before. All media and opinion polls were predicting that Paul Johnson would win. He was emerging as the stronger candidate. He had seen Sarah Baker's statement, where she had referred to the news article on Paul being involved in drug trade. Paul had very cleverly managed to set aside the said statement.

At around 11 a.m., when he was watching a TV news channel, his phone rang. He looked at his phone; it was a new number, a landline number. He decided to answer the call.

'Hello?'

'Am I talking to Mr Rahul Mehra?' asked a sophisticated voice from the other end.

'Who is this?'

'My name is Aneesh Nair. I'm the Joint Secretary of the Government of India. I'd like to speak with Mr Rahul Mehra.'

'Yes, Rahul Mehra speaking.'

'I'm sorry, sir, for disturbing you but do you have a few minutes to spare? I need to confirm something. It's slightly urgent.'

'Yes, please?'

'Were you the chief of NCB, Mr Mehra?'

'Once upon a time, yes,' Rahul replied, cautiously.

'I need to meet you urgently, Mr Mehra.'

'What for?'

'It's for an official purpose. And it's really urgent. We need your help.'

'My help? I didn't get you, Mr Nair.'

'Mr Mehra, 'I'll explain all details when we meet. Please don't mind the urgency. You're a former bureaucrat; you'll understand that exigencies do occur.'

'This is strange,' Rahul objected.

'Sir, please, we need your help. It's the government that needs you. I'm not calling on personal capacity.'

'Okay,' Rahul gave in reluctantly, realizing that it would be rude to refuse a meeting.

'Thank you so much. I'm sending my office car to your address. The driver will bring you here to the ministry office.'

'Which ministry?'

'External Affairs.'

'At what time do you expect me to be there, Mr Nair?'

'Sir, the car will be at your residence, say around 1 p.m. Please give me your address.'

Rahul gave him the address. The phone line went dead. For the life of him, Rahul couldn't comprehend any possible reason as to what the MEA wanted from him.

At 1.45 p.m., Rahul was sitting with Aneesh, at the latter's cabin. Aneesh had offered him tea and coffee, which Rahul had politely declined.

'I'm really sorry, Mr Mehra, to have troubled you.'

'It's okay. What's the urgency? What sort of help are you expecting from me, Mr Nair? I'm an old retired official.'

'Mr Mehra, I'll not waste much time on formalities. I've come to know that you have been contacted by an American intelligence agent recently. Is that right?'

'Please continue.'

Rahul had been the chief of NCB and that post was equivalent to that of Additional Secretary, a post higher to Joint Secretary. He was used to talking to officials working in ministries.

Sir, I'll not keep you in the dark; I'll place all my cards on the table. That agent, perhaps, asked you to give evidence in a drug case which was made long back, when you were the NCB chief. Drugs were seized at that time but the detained men were perhaps released. You got to know that the drug

Chapter 31

racket, which was busted, was, in fact, run by a drug lord named Paul. To be exact, Paul Johnson. The American intelligence agencies don't want a drug trader to be the president of the USA but Paul Johnson has been able to gather the momentum in his favour. American intelligence agencies need substantial evidence to use against Paul Johnson, so that the other candidate, Sarah Baker, wins the election. You know up to this stage.'

Aneesh looked at Rahul for some reaction. Rahul kept silent, returned Aneesh's gaze steadily. Aneesh continued.

'Now, when you met the American agent in Delhi, he communicated the details of your conversation to his headquarters in Virginia. I'm not aware how it was communicated, but Russian intelligence agencies intercepted the said information. One officer from Russian External Affairs contacted me and narrated the whole sequence of events. I came to know of your meeting with the American agent through the Russian officer. Do you know what is the purpose behind the Russians to tell us all this?'

'I'm sure you'll tell me, Mr Nair. Please continue.'

'The Russians want Paul Johnson to become the president of the USA for reasons known to them. They've requested that we should contact you and request you not to give evidence, if any, to the Americans. I was trying to locate you but it took me considerable time to get your contact details.'

'I'm not in hiding, Mr Nair. I'm only living my retired life.'

'Sir, I called you today and I again apologize for inconveniencing you. The reason is firstly to know whether, in fact, there is any evidence against Paul Johnson in your possession.'

'No. I don't have any and I told the same to that American agent too. I thought the issue stood closed.'

'But the American agent is confident that you have some evidence and the Russians are anxious that you may hand it over to the Americans.'

'Mr Nair, I appreciate that you told me all the details, half of which were already known to me. The Russian angle is new. May I put forth a small question?'

'Yes, of course. I'll do my best to reply.'

'What does the Indian government want?'

It was the most valid question coming from a retired senior bureaucrat. Aneesh had gathered some information about Rahul's tenure in NCB. He was a dead honest, loyal and upright officer. It was difficult to influence him. Aneesh said, 'Sir, you have a formidable reputation of being an upright and honest officer.'

'Is that a compliment?'

'Definitely. The Indian government is of the opinion that if you're in possession of any evidence, it may kindly be handed over to our government. It is neither to be given to the Americans nor to the Russians.'

'So that you can use it for diplomatic gains.'

'To some extent, yes.'

'Whom would our government like to see as the next US president?'

'That is not of the concern of our government. We have to take a middle path. We have to strike a balance. Both are superpowers. Our government cannot afford to annoy either of them.'

'Okay. Can I take that the meeting is over?'

'No. No, sir. I know I can trust you. You can also trust us. You're an Indian citizen. You've been a senior government employee. I hope you'll tell us what actually happened that day and thereafter.'

Rahul considered Aneesh's request and thought that there would be nothing wrong in telling what had

Chapter 31

happened. It wasn't a secret, only an official secret. He said, 'Mr Nair, when I came back from the minister's house that day, I held a meeting with my officers. My officers had been able to unlock one of the laptops. They were able to get the password. I asked them to copy the contents of the laptop and one of the officers handed me the same on a pen drive. The laptops were returned. I didn't reveal this part to the American agent.'

'Do you have the pen drive?'

'No,' Rahul sighed deeply. 'I had forgotten everything but the day I met the American agent, I recollected that the contents of one of the laptops were copied on a pen drive. I was in the habit of keeping copies of all sensitive documents. I used to bring CDs or pen drives to my residence. I have since made all efforts to trace the pen drive at all possible places, but unfortunately, I'm unable to locate it.'

'And you don't have any idea what exactly was there in the laptops?'

'No. I haven't seen it. You know, after two days I was transferred and posted to London. I had less than five years left for retirement. I got retired while I was in London.'

Aneesh considered all this. He was certain Rahul had told him the truth. That meant there was no evidence of the case showing any involvement of Paul Johnson. He looked at Rahul and said, 'Thank you, sir. If you happen to get hold of the pen drive, will you please let us know?'

'Yes, I will.'

'One more request. Don't tell the Americans.'

'I haven't told them anything. I don't want to involve myself in any controversy.'

'And will you allow us to see the contents of the said pen drive?'

'Provided I find it!'

'Sure, sir. My car will drop you back. Thanks once again.'

Rahul stood up to leave. Aneesh suddenly asked, 'Sir, just out of curiosity, how come your name doesn't appear on pension records?'

Rahul smiled and said, 'They changed my name from Rahul to Rakul in the passport as well as in my transfer orders. All my pension papers were made in the name of Rakul Mehra in London.'

Rahul came out of the MEA. The car was waiting for him.

******

Ayesha was waiting. She had asked the receptionist to let her know when Sheela Nair arrives. Sheela was late that day. When she entered office, it was 11.30 a.m. When Ayesha got the message, she hurried to Sheela's cabin.

'Good morning, ma'am.'

'Good morning, please have a seat.'

Sheela was expecting Ayesha because she had called her in the morning to get Rahul's contact details.

'Ma'am, Mr Anand Banerjee had called. He said that he had been trying to contact you since yesterday.'

Sheela looked at her younger colleague and asked, 'Ayesha, what's your opinion of Anand?'

'He's our literary agent, for years now, and is an intelligent, nice person and ...'

'And?'

'Your close friend,' answered Ayesha, wondering why Sheela was asking her such questions.

'That's okay. I'm asking, what do *you* think of him. Forget that he's my friend. Tell me frankly,' Sheela encouraged her.

'I wouldn't like to offend you, ma'am.'

'That means you don't like him.'

Chapter 31

'Yes, ma'am, I don't like him,' replied Ayesha, looking and feeling awkward.

'As a woman?' Sheela prodded her further.

'As a woman.'

'Why?'

'I don't think he's trustworthy, ma'am.'

That was perhaps what Sheela wanted to hear. She closed her eyes for a while and said, 'Thank you, Ayesha. You've relieved me of a burden.'

'I didn't get you.'

'See ... I was tempted to share with him all that Ashutosh had told us but there was something holding me back from telling him, despite the fact that he's a close friend. I had the same feeling that he may not be trustworthy.'

'I thought you wanted to get Rahul Mehra's details for him only,' Ayesha was puzzled.

'No,' Sheela replied, paused momentarily and then said, 'not for him.'

Ayesha was hesitant. Still, she said, 'I know you would never contact Rahul Mehra yourself. You needed it for someone. It's obvious.'

'You're right. I talked to Aneesh yesterday. He wanted the contact details. Keep it to yourself.'

'Did you meet him?' Ayesha asked, all agog.

'He spent the night at my place,' Sheela said, smiling.

'Nice to hear that, ma'am.'

'Do you think Aneesh is trustworthy?'

'One hundred per cent.'

Both Sheela and Ayesha grinned at each other and then broke into laughter.

Chapter – 24

Sarah Baker was feeling uncomfortable. She had just received an envelope through a carrier at her hotel in Portland. She had arrived in the city late last night and was scheduled for campaigning there. The envelope contained a short note asking her to speak about Samuel Garcia of Columbia:

> *You'll get a newspaper by 12 noon, wherein will be a news article about Samuel Garcia, who is a drug trader in Columbia. The article will be titled:*
>
> *'What is the relationship between Paul Johnson and Samuel Garcia?'*

Sarah was an academician; she was highly educated and felt that she was being made to give disgraceful statements against her opponent.

******

Earlier, Steve had concentrated on one name – Samuel Garcia – in Ajeet Singh's statement. He had asked his staff to dig around for information on Samuel Garcia. They found that Samuel Garcia was very much active and was handling the drug business on his own. He had powerful friends in Columbia. He was stated to not have travelled outside Columbia. But that was all; no other information could be found on Samuel Garcia. Steve could have used Ajeet Singh's statement in totality but it had an inherent risk of informing Paul Johnson that the laptop had been unlocked. That would be dangerous. So, Steve decided to just drop the name of Samuel Garcia as step two.

Chapter 31

He was apprised that Rahul Mehra had been called to the MEA. This was significant. It wasn't possible to know what exactly was the purpose but he was certain that Rahul's telephone calls and email would be under the surveillance of the Indian intelligence agencies. He informed Justin and cautioned him to be careful.

******

Sarah had received a copy of the newspaper by 11.45 a.m. Her speech was scheduled at 1 p.m. It was a different newspaper and not the earlier one in which the first news had appeared.

There were the usual commitments and action proposals by the party that were announced during the speech. She had by now learnt the major points, which she was required to recite at almost all places. At the end of her speech, she took out the newspaper from her folder and waved it in front of the audience.

'Here is another news article about a drug trader from Columbia and the article questions Paul Johnson's relationship with Samuel Garcia, the drug trader. I'm requesting all media personnel. Please don't come to me asking for clarifications. I've no comments. I've no idea of the authenticity of such a disgraceful article. If my media friends want any clarification, please go and ask Paul and I may kindly be excused. I'm not in the race to throw dirt on anyone.'

She ended her speech. There was pandemonium in the audience. The media personnel scrambled to get copies of the newspaper in which this story had been printed.

Steve was listening to Sarah's speech in his office. Smart way to wriggle out, he thought, pleased.

******

Peter Avilov called up Aneesh Nair, 'Hello, Aneesh.'

'Good evening, Peter,' responded Aneesh.

'Any news?' asked the Russian diplomat.

'I've good news for you, Peter. I had a meeting with Rahul Mehra the other day. You were right, he did meet the American agent. He told me everything.'

'Did he tell them ... the Americans ... anything?'

'No. He said he was in possession of no evidence.'

'Is he actually in possession of any evidence?'

That was tricky. Aneesh replied, 'Yes.'

Peter remained silent. After a while, he enquired, 'What sort of evidence?'

'He told me his team had been successful in unlocking one of the two laptops. Rahul got the contents copied on a pen drive before returning the laptops.'

'That's dangerous!'

'But since it happened many years ago, he has misplaced the pen drive.'

Peter relaxed somewhat. 'Has he told the same story to the American agent?'

'No. He simply told them that he has nothing in his possession and that the laptops couldn't be unlocked.'

'That's a relief.'

'I've asked him to try and locate the pen drive and if he's successful, he's to give it to us, the Indian government.'

'Will I be allowed to see the contents?'

'Look, our promise was to stop handing over the evidence to the Americans. That much I'm assuring, Peter.' Aneesh's tone was grave and non-committal.

'Is he reliable?' Peter persisted.

'Yes. He's a typical government employee, devoted to his country.'

Chapter 31

'Thank you. Did you hear about Sarah Baker's latest speech?'

Aneesh answered in the negative, adding, 'You see, I'm not following all that diligently.'

'She again waved a newspaper before the audience and gave a reference to Samuel Garcia of Columbia.'

'Who's he?'

'I don't know,' admitted Peter, sounding frustrated. 'The news article says he's a drug trader in Columbia and perhaps there's some relationship between him and Paul Johnson.'

'She's treading carefully,' observed Aneesh.

'It's the CIA. They'll try everything to tarnish Paul Johnson'.

'Not everything. It's only his nexus with the narcotics mafia.'

'That was his past,' Peter said swiftly.

'But the past does tend to haunt one, repeatedly.'

'You're right. Will you please apprise me of any development?'

'Sure, what about that anti-aircraft defence equipment?'

'We're working on it. I'll be personally coming with a blueprint.'

'Okay.'

******

Instead of calling, Anand Banerjee visited Spellers to meet Sheela, but she had left office early that day. Anand went to Sanjeev's cabin.

'Hello, Sanjeev!'

'Oh, hello,' Sanjeev smiled and got up.

'How's everything?'

'Fine, sir. What brings you to our office? Please be seated,' Sanjeev offered politely.

'I'd come to meet Sheela but I'm told she left early,' said Anand sitting down.

'Yes, sir. Would you like some tea or coffee?'

'No, no, nothing. Tell me, what's new?'

'The author of *The Grass*, Ashutosh, had come the other day and met Sheela Ma'am.'

'That's good. He himself took an appointment?'

'No, Ayesha brought him and introduced him to Sheela Ma'am.'

'So, have you decided to publish that book?'

Sanjeev kept silent.

'What happened? You were looking for him, weren't you ... for publishing rights,' Anand continued.

'Yes, but I wasn't here at that time and hence, not present at the meeting. I have no idea how the meeting went.'

Anand smelt a rat: Sanjeev wasn't ready to talk; Sheela wasn't answering his calls. He enquired, 'Did anybody ask Ashutosh about the mystery of the last chapter?'

'Sir, I told you, I've no clue – I wasn't at the meeting. I don't know whether this point was discussed or not. Speaking with Sheela Ma'am regarding this is the best,' Sanjeev said feebly.

'Okay,' Anand said, pressing his lips in displeasure. He got up slowly and left Sanjeev's cabin.

******

The second apartment on the first floor where Rahul lived was unoccupied. It was taken on rent by two youths, both bachelors, who hailed from some place in western Uttar Pradesh. Rahul noticed the apartment was being cleaned, swept and given a fresh coat of paint to make it livable. In

Chapter 31

another three days, the two youths would come with their luggage and start living there.

Both these young men were in fact deputed by Indian intelligence to keep a watch on Rahul. They also fixed a camera at their own entrance at such an angle that the main door of Rahul's flat was also visible. They were instructed not to interfere with any of Rahul's movements whatsoever. Nor should anyone in the neighbourhood realize that Rahul was being watched. They were told that there might be a possibility of surveillance by some agency. They both were asked to be on the lookout for such an agency, if it was there.

So, Rahul Mehra now had neighbours.

******

Paul Johnson got down at Tacoma International Airport at night. Michael Taylor, the mayor of King County, was there to receive him at the airport, and after greeting Paul, they headed to the Bellevue Club Hotel. Paul's schedule for campaigning was fixed for the next day at the Bellevue.

Michael, who was driving, looked at Paul Johnson and said, 'Sir, have you heard Sarah's statement?'

'Which one? Is it something new?'

'The same trick. She waved a newspaper, with an article about a Columbian drug dealer, Samuel Garcia, questioning his relationship with you.'

Alarm bells started ringing in Paul's mind. Samuel Garcia used to be his right hand in the drug trade at one time. Samuel handled all the work. He was a sort of front man. Ever since Paul dissociated himself from the drug trade, Samuel was handling the business on his own. Paul wondered how Samuel's name popped up now. Someone was selectively leaking such information in the newspapers and conveying the same to Sarah.

Clearly, an attempt was being made to tarnish him, an attempt was being made to reverse public opinion, which at the moment was in his favour. Feeling both annoyed and worried, he said to Michael, 'This is bad. She mustn't stoop so low. Employing such tactics while campaigning for the presidential election is outrageous.'

'Yes, sir, something has got to be done.'

Paul concurred silently. He, however, asked, 'Will the media be there at the hotel now?'

'No, the media came but they were told that you're coming late tonight. They dispersed.'

'They may again come.'

'Not tonight, sir, hopefully,' the mayor assured him.

'But this has to be dealt with strongly.'

In half an hour, they reached the hotel. Some supporters who had been waiting for him, greeted him enthusiastically. Paul waved to them and then excused himself on the pretext of being tired, and went to his room. Once in his room alone, he contemplated on what was happening. He was sure it wouldn't stop here. In another week or two, something more might come up. Officially, Paul had no past record of being involved in the drug trade. He had been careful enough. But who could be behind all this? Was it someone from the drug trade itself? That didn't seem possible because in the drug trade, no one speaks against anyone. It was an unwritten law. Was there some enforcement agency? That too seemed impossible because Paul was well versed in the workings of enforcement agencies. They never leak information which was on their record. And he was certain that he was nowhere on the record of any enforcement agency. The first news article could possibly have been a rumour but bringing in the name of Samuel Garcia meant someone *knew*. Oh God! He found himself praying for the next four months to pass without any further calamity.

Chapter 31

Pacing up and down in his room, he desperately wished he could contact someone from the trade because their intelligence network was perhaps better than any official intelligence agency. He was feeling helpless in a way because he was cut off. But one wrong move would spell disaster for him. Someone out there was waiting for him to do exactly that. He was sure that the details of his telephone calls and emails could be made public. So many security or intelligence agencies were used to keeping watch on prominent candidates, as either of these prominent candidates would become the next president of the USA.

Chapter – 25

At 10 a.m., Rahul's mobile phone rang; it was Justin Brown. Rahul had met him only once before, and all this time there hadn't been any meeting nor any call. This call was unexpected. He picked up the phone.

'Hello?'

'Good morning, Mr Mehra.'

'Good morning, Mr Brown.'

'Sir, can we meet?'

'What's happened? Anything urgent?'

'I'd prefer to meet you in person, Mr Mehra. It's important from your point of view.'

'Okay. Same place, where we met last time?'

'Yes, sir. Can we fix it for 12 noon today?'

'Okay, I'll be there,' Rahul assured him and disconnected.

Justin was aware of the possibility of Rahul's phone being tapped. He couldn't take any chances.

At about noontime, they were sitting face to face in a small coffee shop at Connaught place.

'I'm sorry I had to disturb you.'

'It's okay. What is it?'

Justin placed an envelope on the table. It was sealed. Gently sliding it towards Rahul, he said, 'This is for you, Mr Mehra.'

'What's in it?' Rahul was intrigued.

'This has all the documents of the case you made ten years back in NCB – the last case.'

'The documents?' Rahul repeated, surprised.

Chapter 31

'Yes. Don't open it here,' Justin hastily cautioned as Rahul was about to do so. 'You can take it. It has one seizure memo and four statements given by different persons, which were recorded.'

Rahul's curiosity was piqued; he tried to recollect. The file was taken over by the minister but before going to the minister's office, he had asked Malini, his assistant, to take photocopies. He never went back to office that day.

'From where have you got these?'

'Mr Mehra, I'll not tell a lie. Our office in Virginia scrutinized your emails. It was found in those emails, sent by one Malini.'

'You looked into my emails?' Rahul felt his temper rising.

'I'm sorry for intruding on your privacy. But we're interested only in finding something against Paul Johnson. I told you earlier too.'

'Is that how you work?' he snapped in quiet fury.

'All intelligence agencies work like this. Their job is to collect intelligence. You were chief of NCB. The NCB too looked into call details and emails. That is how we get information.'

'But they look into details of suspects! Do you consider me a suspect?' Rahul tried to control himself.

'Sir, I'm really sorry. But just hear me out – I needn't have told you this, nor handed over these documents to you. You would have never known about this. At least, we're honest,' Justin said earnestly.

Somewhat pacified, Rahul said, 'You're honest as far as your own work is concerned.'

'True. To some extent.'

'Why are you giving this to me? It's the other way round. You're giving documents to me while you've been expecting me to give you some documents.'

'Mr Mehra, you hadn't seen these documents because you hadn't opened that particular email. It was sent to you ten years back. Otherwise, it wouldn't have been possible to retrieve such old emails.'

'Yes, I stopped going through such emails. In fact, I lost all interest once I was asked to shut the case.'

'These are very important documents, Mr Mehra.' Justin tapped the envelope as he spoke.

'I'll see these later. Is there anything else you would like to say?'

'Yes,' Justin said softly, after considering for some time. He continued, 'You told me the other day that the laptops couldn't be unlocked. There's a statement in these documents, where a person was confronted with the contents of one laptop and he admitted that one laptop couldn't be opened while the other one was opened, as he had the password.'

Rahul leant back in his chair, his face inscrutable, his eyes looking straight into Justin's, 'Aah, so this is to make me realize that I lied on that day. Tell me, Mr Brown, am I under any obligation to tell you anything at all or to meet you?'

'No, sir. You're not under any obligation. And please, I haven't come to embarrass you, or challenge you. It's very simple. Once you go through the documents, you may recollect something else.'

'Do these documents not serve your purpose?'

'I don't know. But I'm given to understand that our chief is looking for more evidence.'

'Thank you, Mr Brown. I'll go through these documents.'

'Sir, one more thing. You're being watched.'

'Watched? By who?' Rahul sat up straight, immediately alert.

'I don't know but two people who have just moved into the apartment next to yours are watching you.'

Chapter 31

'Are they your staff?'

'Sir, I wouldn't have told you had they been ours. My headquarters only sent me an email that if I communicate with you, I should avoid telephone calls and emails. Both of these may be under surveillance.'

'You're quite updated, I must say.'

'I'm not alone, sir. I'm part of a system. What I wanted to tell you is that next time I'll not make a call. We normally use a carrier, a private carrier, to deliver the message. That's the safest.'

Rahul thought for a while and then asked, 'And if I have to communicate, what shall I do?'

'Sir, simply give me a missed called whenever you need a carrier. One boy will come to collect the message.'

'That's great.'

Justin was about to get up, when Rahul gestured him to remain seated. He ordered another round of coffee, without asking Justin.

'I would like to tell you something, Mr Brown.'

'Sure,' Justin said, surprised.

'I've some information which your chief may relish.'

'What?'

'The details of our first meeting were sent by you to your headquarters or your chief or whoever. I'm not aware of your mode of communication. But that communication of yours was intercepted by Russian intelligence.' Rahul paused to look at Justin's reaction.

'No!' Justin exclaimed in dismay.

'Yes, it's confirmed. They have my name. They know why I was contacted.'

'That is a huge lapse on our part.'

'Now, one Russian diplomat had approached the Indian government to request me not to give evidence, if any, to you – the Americans.'

When Justin had walked in for the meeting with Rahul, he had felt both pride and a sense of accomplishment hoping that he would surprise Rahul by handing over the case papers, which he had never seen. But now his face went white, and he was nervous and horrified. Rahul had not only surprised him but made him realize that they, the American intelligence, were not the best in the world! The Russians should have been the last of all to whom such news should have travelled.

Rahul looked at Justin, taking in his state of shock. Concerned, he said, 'Mr Brown, I never intended to upset you. It was meant for your information so that you may adopt whatever corrective measures you consider suitable.'

'Thank you, sir. I'm grateful to you for sharing such vital information.'

'Things have become complicated for me. You want evidence, while the Russians don't want me to part with any evidence!' Rahul said and laughed. He continued, 'The problem is, where is the evidence? I don't have any evidence.'

'Sir, may I ask one question?'

'Yes,' Rahul was feeling relaxed now, while Justin was still trying to grapple with what he'd just heard.

'Sir, whatever you've just told me is hopefully from an authentic source?'

'Definitely, Mr Brown. The Indian government had summoned me. I was briefed about the issue. I gave the same answer that I've no evidence and there's no question of handing it over to anyone.'

They had finished their coffee. Rahul patted Justin and said, 'Don't take it to heart, Mr Brown. These are professional lapses. These do occur. I've been a part of all this intelligence gathering ... I know.'

Justin simply smiled and bade him goodbye.

******

Chapter 31

Rahul, as usual, took the stairs to reach the first floor. The door of the apartment next to his apartment was closed. He glanced about him carefully, unobtrusively. He spotted a camera focused towards the door of his apartment. It seemed Justin was correct. He unlocked his door and went in.

Once inside his apartment, Rahul, as a precautionary measure, looked around. Though it wasn't likely, he wanted to be certain there wasn't any tiny camera hidden at some place, to catch any activity in his room. No, he didn't spot anything.

He sat down and opened the envelope and started reading all the five documents – one seizure memo and the four statements. It was Ajeet Singh's statement that caught his attention. He read it twice. It had been well-recorded by Lalit Gaur, one of his junior officers.

So, the Americans have come to know that one of the laptops was opened, he thought.

He saw the name Samuel Garcia. He also saw the name Paul – an incomplete name mentioned in the statement. He couldn't help cursing himself. Had he taken the stand at that time, the investigation would have gone a long way. But it had been stopped midway. He again felt saddened after a long period. I alone am responsible, Rahul thought.

That morning, on a news channel, Rahul had seen that one more article had appeared in some newspaper in the USA, mentioning the name Samuel Garcia. Rahul was convinced that this was Justin's boss's handiwork. From his own experiences, Rahul knew that such news articles wouldn't affect public sentiment but were sufficient to irritate Paul Johnson. The American intelligence might expect Paul to make a wrong move out of frustration. That could be the only possibility.

****

This time, Aneesh took the initiative. He called Sheela; it was 4 p.m.

'Hello?' he said when he heard the call connecting with the other end.

'How are you?' There was a pleasant ring in Sheela's voice.

'What a lovely voice!'

'Tell me, why have you called? I don't think you intend to spend another night at my place,' she teased.

'No. I don't.'

'So then ...?'

'I want you to spend the night at my place. I'm not sure whether you would like it or not – it's a small house, as you well know.'

'No, I don't like that house,' she said truthfully, then thought for a moment and said laughingly, 'you don't have Amma at your place. Who will make dinner?'

'We can have dinner outside, at a place that you fancy?'

'No, not outside.'

'You don't want to be seen with Aneesh Nair!' he exclaimed.

She ignored him and said instead, 'It's best that you come to my place. I'll call Amma right now and she'll keep dinner ready.'

'Yeah, I'll come.'

'That's what you wanted to hear, isn't it?' she couldn't resist poking him.

'Great! See you soon,' Aneesh said cheerfully and disconnected.

Sheela, sitting at her desk, was smiling away. The ex-husband seemed to be getting interested in her. Or was it the other way round? Was Sheela the one who was getting interested in him?

Chapter 31

They enjoyed the delicious dinner that Amma had rustled up and spent the night together at Sheela's place. They talked a lot about their days together in the past but none touched upon the reasons for their separation.

In the morning, while having tea, Sheela asked, 'Did you meet Rahul Mehra?'

'Yes. He's a nice old man.'

'What did he say?'

'He said he had no evidence, that it had happened a long way back and that he didn't even remember the facts properly.'

Aneesh didn't tell her about the Russian's interest in Rahul. Nor did he tell her that Rahul had a pen drive which had got misplaced. He didn't consider it proper to share these things with her at this juncture.

Chapter – 26

The next morning, Michal Taylor informed the media that Paul Johnson would be speaking at a gathering and he would definitely respond to Sarah Baker's statement, which she had made the previous day.

The crowd that had turned up to hear Paul's speech, thus naturally expected him to clarify his stand on Sarah's latest statement about him. Paul didn't disappoint them.

He brought up this matter at the end of his speech. 'My dear fellow citizens, a new trend seems to have started … that of tarnishing the image of the opponent. There's a known terrorist in another country. I name him and question you to tell me what's your relationship with him. Everybody here will say "No" in unison. Why? Because you have no relationship! Do you have to justify that you have no relationship? You need not. You are all peace-loving citizens. If there is some Samuel Garcia out in some country dealing in drugs, do I have to justify my relationship? Tell me … Yes or No.'

The audience chorused in one voice, 'No!'

Paul Johnson smiled.

Michal Taylor smiled.

The media personnel smiled.

The message was clear. All such news were nothing but rumours.

As Michael drove Paul back to the hotel, he informed him that one Donald Chen wanted to meet him and that he had fixed an appointment at 1 p.m. at the hotel itself.

'Who is Donald Chen?' Paul asked, unable to recollect this person.

Chapter 31

'Sir, he's a very important man.'

'We don't have the time to meet anyone now, Michael.'

'I couldn't deny him an appointment simply because he's a member of Super PAC. He's a very rich man ... he owns about twenty-seven casinos all around the US. Two of the casinos are here on the highway to Vancouver. He has influential friends in the judiciary as well as among politicians. One cannot deny him this meeting. Just give him twenty minutes, sir. It's vital that you meet him. Such individuals cannot be ignored.'

'Okay,' nodded Paul. 'Let's see what he has to say.'

In US, Political Action Committees or PACs, pool campaign contributions from every member and donate these funds to campaigns, sometimes for the candidates and sometimes against the candidates. Super PACs were stated to be on a different pedestal altogether as unlike the traditional PACs, the Super PACs could accept unlimited contribution from individuals, unions and corporations for the purpose of making independent expenditure. Super PACs were made possible by a couple of judicial decisions and while Super PAC members themselves were not allowed to directly engage in campaigns, it was well within the law for them and the candidate to discuss campaign strategies and tactics.

At 1 p.m., Donald Chen entered Paul's hotel room.

Extending his hand, Donald introduced himself and said, 'Sir, I'm contributing funds for your campaigns through a Super PAC.'

'Thank you, Mr Chen. Michael was telling me about you,' Paul shook hands with him, and gestured him to be seated. 'Tell me, Mr Chen, what brings you here?'

'Sir, public opinion is in your favour. We're quite hopeful. The opinion polls are also predicting a win for you.'

'I'm grateful to all of you for supporting me. I'm working hard not to disappoint well-wishers like you,' Paul said charmingly, smiling all the time.

Donald smiled and leant back as if relaxing, and said, 'Sir, I'm a businessman. You, too, are a businessman. We always put money on a winning horse. We're not here for any charity. At least, not me.'

'Yes, me too.'

'Mr Johnson, there have been two adverse news articles against you, particularly the last one …'

'You mean the one questioning my relationship with Samuel Garcia?'

'Yes, sir.'

'Mr Chen, do you personally know any person by the name of Samuel Garcia, who deals in the drug trade?'

Donald looked at Paul and answered hesitantly, 'No one.'

'Mr Chen, if you open Facebook, you'll probably find hundreds, if not thousands, of Samuel Garcias. Do we know what they do? There may be people named Donald Chen. They may not be a successful businessman like you; there may be corrupt Donald Chens too. I fail to understand why there's so much fuss,' Paul finished confidently.

'Sir, because you're fighting an election; others aren't. You're going to be the next president of the USA! Your name being associated with a narcotics man does matter.'

Paul kept silent.

Donald continued, 'Sir, there're whispers among members of the Super PAC. They feel that even a slight shift in the percentage of voters towards Sarah Baker might affect the results.'

'I can understand your concern, Mr Chen,' Paul said seriously.

Chapter 31

'Sir, you must be aware that the Super PACs are a major source of funding for campaigns. In your case, it's around thirty-eight per cent of the total spendings. It's a big amount.'

'Are you warning me?'

'Mr Johnson, I've told you, I'm a businessman. I've already donated a big amount to the Super PAC. I would always want you to win. All members of Super PACs would want so. I've come with a request ... it's a personal request. Please take some steps so that such adverse reports in the media are avoided.'

'Sure. Your managers and mine can sit together and plan a strategy.'

'Yes, I'll put up the proposal strongly before the committee.'

'Thank you, Mr Chen. I appreciate your concern.'

Donald stood up and shook hands with Paul and left. Paul couldn't help cursing his past. The other members of Super PACs might also raise the same issue. Such a possibility was there. It was an indirect attack and he agreed with Donald Chen that it had to be dealt with effectively.

Paul called his two managers and asked them if he could take a two-day break from campaigning. He wanted to mull over the situation with a clear head and get in touch with any of his old associates in Columbia. He was certain that not only would they be able to find out the source of such leaked news, but they would also know how to stop it. The managers looked at the schedule for the following week and suggested that he take a break in the coming weekend.

******

Rahul called Aneesh and fixed up a meeting; Aneesh told him that an official vehicle would wait for him at his residence to bring him to the ministry's office. An official vehicle had its own unique advantage: one wasn't subjected to the rigorous security checks when entering the MEA. Aneesh greeted Rahul on his reaching the ministry's office.

'Hello, sir.'

'Hello, Mr Nair.'

'Pleasure to meet you again, sir,' Aneesh said, pulling up a chair for Rahul.

'Thank you. Any update?' Rahul asked, sitting down.

'Nothing new,' said Aneesh as he sat down in his chair.

'Did the Russian diplomat contact you?'

'Yes, I told him you have no documents and that you cannot recollect much about the case.'

Rahul handed him the envelope that Justin had given him.

'What's this?'

'Open it, take a look,' Rahul invited him.

Aneesh opened the envelope to find some documents, coming to about twenty-eight pages. He started reading the documents and his excitement grew with every document that he completed. He took about half an hour to read all the pages. Finally, he looked up at Rahul and said, 'These relate to that case of Paul Johnson.'

'You must have seen his name appearing at a few places.'

'Yes, yes.'

'These are the documents that I got.'

'You were able to trace these documents?'

'No,' Rahul shook his head. 'The American agent handed these over to me.'

Aneesh was taken by surprise. 'How come?'

'They retrieved my old emails. These were found in one of the emails.'

'But why have these been handed over to you, sir? They need it themselves.' Aneesh was baffled.

Chapter 31

'They've used it. See, one person by the name of Samuel Garcia has been mentioned in a statement. It was in the news the other day. Sarah Baker referred to this name – Samuel Garcia.'

'Yes, I saw the news. So, they picked up the name from here,' Aneesh Nair mused, tapping the documents.

'They handed it over to me because it was evident from these documents that one of the laptops was unlocked.'

'That means they still feel that there might be more evidence.'

'Perhaps.'

'What happened to the pen drive, sir? Were you able to find it?'

'No.'

'Can I share these with the Russian diplomat? I will do so only if you give your consent.'

Rahul looked at Aneesh and smiled.

'You can take these back, sir,' Aneesh said.

'I have copies. These are for you. Can you extract some diplomatic mileage through these?'

'Yes and no. They're smart.'

'Anyway, that's your outlook. I just wanted to apprise you of this new development. I know these documents cannot be termed as conclusive. But yes, these are sufficient to create problems for Paul Johnson … as an irritant.'

'Thank you, sir. I'll talk to my seniors and discuss how these are to be used, if to be used at all.'

Rahul got up, smiled and said, 'Why have you deputed personnel to keep me under surveillance?'

Aneesh looked a bit nervous. He kept silent for a while and then said slowly, 'Sir, they're not keeping a watch on you. There's no need of that. I had told our staff to ask local authorities to provide you with security.'

'If I say, I don't need the security?'

'They'll be withdrawn.'

'Better do that, then. Don't make me uncomfortable, Mr Nair.'

'That'll be done,' Aneesh assured the elderly gentleman.

Rahul also wanted to talk about the surveillance on his phone and emails but he wasn't sure if he should. He was aware that any discussion on that would give an indication that he was being informed. So, he eventually avoided that.

******

Steve was informed that Paul was taking a two-day break and was going to spend these two days in some island, near Seattle. He asked his agents to keep a watch on him. Steve was certain Paul would try to contact someone in person or telephonically, when in isolation. He asked his agents to be alert and update him on the details of his vacation.

Steve also got the news that the Russians had come to know of the details of meetings with Rahul and that they were using their clout in the Indian government so that Rahul wouldn't reveal anything to the Americans. That was disturbing, very disturbing. Whatever little information he could obtain about Rahul was that his weakness lay in his loyalty to his own government. The other indication of this information was that the Russians wanted Paul as the next president of the USA. By the looks of it, they seemed to be supporting Paul.

Chapter – 27

A couple of days after meeting Aneesh, it occurred to Rahul that his passport was due for renewal; when he had returned home from his last visit to the USA, he had noticed that his passport would expire in the next eight months. Six months had passed. He thought of applying for renewal before the expiry date. He opened his cupboard. There was a small locker on the left side of his cupboard, where he would keep some cash and important documents. His passport was also there. He pulled at the small knob of the locker only to realize that it was locked. The key of the locker was normally placed under the shirts on the right side. He looked there, lifting the shirt. No, it wasn't there. He started removing his shirts, thinking that the key could have got misplaced somewhere in the pile of shirts. While doing so, by chance his hands lightly moved a blue blazer that was hanging with his other coats. Again, his hands brushed against it. When his hand again came into contact with the blazer, he felt something in one of the outer pockets of the blue blazer. He put his hand inside the pocket to see what could be there. It was a pen drive. He took it out, staring at it for a few seconds and then all of a sudden, he realized that this could be the one he had been looking for all these days. Perhaps he had worn this blazer to office that day and when Lalit had handed him the pen drive, he had absent-mindedly dropped it in his pocket. It had been there since then, over these many years!

Barely able to contain his excitement, Rahul hastily inserted it to his laptop and clicked on the folders in the pen drive. The emails were there; the trail mails were there. He kept looking. Three names were coming up repeatedly; these were Yunus, Samuel Garcia and Paul. He continued perusing, scrutinizing every detail, every file, every document. He abruptly stopped at one stage: he read 'Johnson' along with 'Paul'. His eyes widened; he checked the date. It was one of the oldest trail mails. He studied the document again and again. 'Paul Johnson' was mentioned at just one place while 'Paul' was mentioned umpteen number of times. The full name at one place clarified the name 'Paul' too. The contents of all the emails were related to details of the supply of drugs and the payments to be received. At one place, there were directions to Samuel Garcia to eliminate the person who was delaying payment on one pretext or the other.

Rahul found that there were two folders. He opened the first one. It had a long list of names, with the contact details of various persons involved in the network. It was quite exhaustive. He smiled; the email addresses and details of the contacts were sufficient to pin down Paul Johnson. This was exactly what the CIA was looking for. He closed the laptop. He wanted to relax and cool down. He sighed; the pen drive with its incriminating evidence had been with him all along and he hadn't been aware of it.

He was in two minds, should he inform Justin? Or should he call Aneesh? He was in a dilemma. And then, there was a third option – remain quiet.

******

Bainbridge was a small island in the state of Washington. Accompanied by his wife, Paul Johnson had checked in at a resort located on that island. They were given a beautiful beach-facing room, surrounded by lush green flora. After spending a couple of hours in the room, Paul went out to the beach. There were two small restaurants and one bar at one side and a large-sized swimming pool on the other.

Chapter 31

He sat down on a beach chair. The sun felt good. He lazily took in the tourists enjoying the sunshine and the children playing about noisily.

An intelligence agent was sitting at one of the restaurants, nibbling at a burger.

Paul settled down in the beach chair, feeling soothed and closed his eyes. However, he suddenly heard footsteps, as if someone was walking up to him. He opened his eyes and started. Donald Chen was standing there, looking at him.

'Oh hello. What a surprise,' Paul said politely, hiding his annoyance.

'Hello, sir.'

'Are you on vacation too, Mr Chen?'

'No, sir, I came here intentionally.'

'With what purpose?' Paul squinted up at him, through half-sleepy eyes.

'To have another meeting with you.'

'You could have waited for two days, Mr Chen, what's so urgent?' This time Paul didn't try to suppress his irritation.

'It's urgent,' he said firmly, looking around for a chair to sit.

There was another chair nearby, and Donald dragged it towards Paul's chair and sat down in it. Reluctantly, Paul drew up his legs and sat upright, facing Donald.

'Sir, I'm sorry for intruding on you like this, on your private trip. But it was imperative that I meet you.'

'Please go on.'

'Perhaps you aren't aware of it ... Most of us aren't. There's a corporation, which is one of the members of our Super PAC. It's owned by two Chinese men. I was told by one of them recently that they're both merely a front. The money is invested by Russians.'

'What?' Paul wondered if he had heard right.

'Yes, the Russians, but that cannot be proved. Don't worry about that. I'm not here to tell you that. Yesterday, I was sitting with those two Chinese. One of them told me in confidence that the Russian intelligence agencies had intercepted a message of the CIA, a few months back.'

Paul chuckled and said, 'You mean Russian intelligence told these Chinese men about that interception? This is unbelievable.'

'Sir, please let me complete. Yes, it was told to them because that message was related to you and the Russian intelligence wanted it to be conveyed to you. It is getting difficult to communicate with you with each passing day.'

'What's the message?' asked Paul, his curiosity piqued.

'An American agent had contacted an ex-chief of NCB in India, who had worked on a drugs case about ten years back. His name is Rahul Mehra.'

'So, how is this connected to me?'

'The American agent was looking for some evidence against you because your name figured in that case at that time. The CIA wants to use that evidence to prevent you from becoming the president. It was also found that the Russians were exerting pressure on the Indian government that no evidence, if any, should fall into the hands of the CIA.' Donald stopped and looked at Paul, concerned.

Paul couldn't recollect the details of that case after so many years. He said, 'I told you the other day, it's nothing but misinformation that's being deliberately spread against me. I'm repeating again, I had nothing to do with drugs.'

'Sir, I'm worried. My money is at stake. And others have also contributed to your campaign. People have faith in you. Your party has faith in you. I hope I'm clear. I came here only because it was convenient to talk to you here.' Donald stood up and said, 'Sir, I wish you all the best.'

He went away, his face impassive. As he walked around the pool and passed by the restaurant, the agent took a photograph of Donald Chen from his mobile.

Chapter 31

Paul tried to recollect the old case that had been prepared in India. He could recollect that he had taken the help of a politician. The case had been closed, the detainees released and laptops returned. The CIA was digging into his past. He tried to satisfy himself that there was nothing in that case to link him, particularly now, after ten years. And, the Russians were helping him. But once that became public, he would invariably lose the elections. Americans would never accept someone who was being helped by the Russians as their president. Such rumours had floated around in earlier elections too but nothing substantial was on record. He realized he had to do something. He wanted to call Samuel Garcia but he couldn't use his phone nor the hotel's phone. All these calls were traceable and now, when he was told that the CIA didn't want him as the president, he would have to be vigilant.

Paul got up from his beach chair and casually strolled to the bar counter that was manned by a young bartender. Seeing him alone, Paul asked, 'Hello, young man, may I use your phone?'

The bartender looked up. He had seen Paul's pictures in newspapers and recognized him immediately. Thrilled, the bartender readily passed him his phone. Paul called Samuel Garcia and strolled a little distance away from the counter. After talking for a few minutes, he returned the phone to the bartender, thanked him and left the beach.

The CIA agent sitting at the restaurant had noted everything. He waited for some time, finished his meal, paid and came out. He took a chair near the bar counter. A couple was standing, waiting for their drinks to be served. The agent waited. When their order was served, the couple sat at the bar counter, making themselves comfortable on the bar stools, and enjoyed their drinks leisurely. The agent remained where he was. After half an hour, the couple left their drinks on the counter and jumped into the swimming pool. The agent got up, went to the bar and ordered a vodka-based cocktail. As the bartender began preparing his order, the agent started checking his pockets, as if looking for something.

The agent said, 'Oh, buddy, I think I've misplaced my phone somewhere. Can you help me?'

'Certainly, sir.'

'Just call on my phone number ... I'll tell you my number ... my phone will be here somewhere. I'll be able to locate it once it rings.'

The agent recited his phone number and the bartender punched the digits on his phone's keypad. The phone was lying on the nearest chair under a towel. The agent immediately picked up his phone from the chair, and returned to the bar counter. He took his cocktail and thanked him. The agent came back to the same chair, took a sip and glanced at his phone. He had got the mobile number from where Paul had made the call. He forwarded Donald Chen's photograph and the bartender's phone number to his office in Virginia.

******

Steve had heard about Donald Chen and was aware that he was one of the contributors to the Super PAC, which was funding Paul's election campaign. His meeting with Paul was not of concern. What was of concern, instead, was that Donald had picked a venue for the meeting where Paul had gone on vacation. He was reported that the meeting would have lasted for about twenty minutes. Next was the call made from the bartender's phone. He had got the number of the person to whom the call was made; it hadn't been difficult to find out the name of that person. That person was Samuel Garcia.

******

Chapter 31

While coming up the stairs, Rahul had observed that the camera outside the next apartment was still there, though the door was locked from outside. At night, he once again peeped and saw the door was still locked. He wasn't sure whether the two men were still occupying the apartment or not.

Chapter – 28

It was Tuesday. Rahul Mehra left his apartment for his usual morning walk. He normally walked for about an hour. That day, Rahul didn't come back after an hour. He didn't come back after two hours. He didn't come back after three hours. He didn't come back that day. The two men were watching through the camera. The door to Rahul's apartment remained locked. They had been asked to shift elsewhere but the instruction to keep a watch on Rahul hadn't been withdrawn. The entire day passed by. The next morning, again, no activity was noticed.

They conveyed to their senior in the Home Department that Rahul hadn't been in his apartment for one whole day and night, nor was he seen anywhere else. Wednesday too passed in the same manner.

******

Aneesh called on Rahul's mobile number. An automated voice informed him that the phone was either switched off or was out of coverage area. Aneesh tried calling him again after two hours. There was no response. Now, he got worried. He called the Home Department and told them to find his whereabouts. The local police questioned the guard sitting on the ground floor of Rahul's building. The guard stated that Rahul hadn't been seen for the last two days. The police enquired from a few regular morning walkers in the park. They too stated that Rahul hadn't come for his walk for the last two days.

Aneesh next sought information from immigration authorities. No person by the name of Rahul Mehra or Rakul Mehra had travelled. Thursday too passed by; Rahul wasn't seen anywhere. His whereabouts were not known.

Chapter 31

The police were asked to register a report of a missing person and conduct an investigation and to do it on top priority. The local police looked into the call details of Rahul's mobile phone. The last call was made on Sunday, to a local number but the person at the other end hadn't answered the call. No call had been placed or received on Monday.

Rahul's disappearance became a matter of concern for Aneesh. He simply couldn't figure out what had happened to Rahul. He hadn't gone out of the country. If he was somewhere within India, why would he switch off his mobile phone. Friday and Saturday came and went. It was five days now. So far, Aneesh had been hopeful but now negative thoughts crowded his mind. Had something unfortunate happened? Had Rahul been killed? *Killed.* The word recurred in his mind. Surely it couldn't be true, but a niggling fear had taken hold of Aneesh – if at all he had been killed. Aneesh felt Rahul had been unnecessarily dragged into the controversy. Aneesh was smitten with guilt: that to some extent, he was responsible for whatever had happened to Rahul.

Directions were given to the police to investigate from that angel too.

******

Peter Avilov arrived at Delhi airport. This time it was an official visit. Due protocol for such a visit was followed, and designated personnel from the Russian embassy were at the airport to welcome him. Arrangements for his two days' stay were made by the embassy in collaboration with the PRO of the MEA. He had a meeting with Aneesh the next morning, in the office of the ministry itself.

On Monday, at 10 a.m., Peter was at Aneesh's cabin. They were both accompanied by three other officers for assistance. The meeting lasted for about an hour. Negotiations were held for finalizing the draft agreement for supply of anti-aircraft defence equipment; changes were suggested from both sides, clauses were added, clauses were deleted. Once these were done, the officers assisting them left, leaving them together.

A peon brought in two coffees. Aneesh and Peter sat down on the sofas for their informal talks. They picked up their coffees.

Peter asked, 'So, what's the news?'

'Rahul Mehra has disappeared.'

'What?' Peter exclaimed.

'Yes,' Aneesh replied, his face grave. 'It has been a week now. We were keeping him under surveillance. He went for his usual morning walk and didn't come back.'

'This is a matter of concern.'

'Yes,' Aneesh said. He took a sip of his coffee and looked at Peter for a while. Both remained quiet for some time.

'Had he got anything on Paul Johnson?' Peter asked.

Aneesh went to his desk, opened the drawer and took out an envelope. He handed it to Peter.

'What's this?' Peter asked, taking the envelope.

'Just see.'

Peter read the documents. These were the same documents that Rahul had given to Aneesh. Peter could see the names of Samuel Garcia and Paul in those documents. When he finished, Peter put these back in the envelope and remarked glumly, 'So, Samuel Garcia's name came from these documents.'

'Apparently.'

'That means Rahul gave these to the American agent.'

'It's the other way round. The American agent retrieved the information from Rahul's emails and took printouts. He handed over these to Rahul.'

Chapter 31

'Why did he give these to Rahul Mehra?' Peter was as surprised as Aneesh had been when Rahul had given him the documents.

'It's obvious. The American agent wanted more information about the contents in the laptops.'

'They want the pen drive?'

'Yes.'

'Has he been able to locate the pen drive? You told me he had misplaced it.'

'Yes, that's right. He couldn't locate it. But I'm worried about him, Peter. I was hoping he would be back within the first couple of days. But now a week has passed. And his phone is switched off.'

'What do you think could have happened?'

'I've got his disappearance investigated. He hasn't gone out of India. I fear either he has been kidnapped and detained somewhere, or he has been killed.'

'Killed?' repeated Peter, stunned.

'That possibility cannot be ruled out. Either it is Paul Johnson's old gang or you people … the Russians.'

'What nonsense!' Peter protested sharply. 'Why would we do that?'

'The reason is simple enough. Eliminate the person and eliminate the possibility of transfer of evidence to the American agency,' Aneesh replied in a clipped tone.

'You're not being fair, Aneesh. Your accusation is insane!'

'Yes, I'm being insane,' Aneesh said bluntly. 'It's because of us that he came into the limelight. Rahul Mehra was a retired person living a peaceful life. You approached me and told me about him. It all started since then. If he's dead … it's really bad. I hold myself responsible for his death.'

'Aneesh, our intelligence agencies do not believe in kidnappings, killings, etc.,' Peter's voice was cold. Then, controlling himself, he continued, 'Their job is to collect intelligence and pass the same to the concerned authorities. Here, in this case, there wasn't even the slightest intelligence so far. I only approached you with a humble request and I'm grateful that you responded with some details. I assure you we'll cooperate to find out the missing man.'

'Our police are making all efforts and I'm hopeful they'll come out with some information shortly.'

'I'm sorry for him. I sincerely wish that he is found unharmed.'

Their formal meeting, as well as their informal conversation, over, the delegates headed by Peter returned to the Russian embassy.

Peter was aware that a message had been conveyed to Paul that the CIA was looking for evidence of Paul's involvement in drugs and that they had contacted Rahul Mehra, an ex-chief of the NCB, in India. Peter wondered if Paul was behind Rahul's disappearance. These drug mafias were dangerous. For them, killings were a part and parcel of their trade.

******

Ayesha was sitting with Sheela and they were discussing the publishing of a new book by an Indian author. Spellers India had already published his last two novels. Ayesha was editing his third manuscript. They were deliberating on the prospects of its popularity. While the earlier two novels had done well, they hadn't set the charts on fire as Spellers had expected.

'Ma'am, in my opinion, we should go ahead. The plot, the storyline and the climax are all good. I've gone through the script. It's gripping.'

As usual, Sheela wasn't interested in the contents.

'Do you know, Ayesha, the last two novels we published barely covered the expenses? Spellers couldn't earn much.'

Chapter 31

'But this happens a number of times. It's a matter of chance. Sometimes, when one novel becomes a bestseller, the earlier ones too start selling.'

'So, you think we should publish it.'

'Yes, ma'am,' Ayesha responded promptly.

'Okay. Just discuss with Shankar also and if he too concurs, go ahead.'

Sheela's phone rang. It was Aneesh. She picked up the phone.

'There's bad news, Sheela,' Aneesh told her.

'What?'

'Rahul Mehra has disappeared.'

Sheela kept quiet; Ayesha was sitting with her.

'Aneesh, we can meet and talk,' Sheela suggested.

'Is there someone …?'

'Yes. You can come home in the evening.'

'It will be our third meeting in a month,' Aneesh reminded her, sounding cheerful.

Sheela smiled, 'Three isn't a big number.'

'Okay then, meeting you at your place.'

They disconnected.

Ayesha, who had inadvertently listened to Sheela's responses, asked, 'Was that Aneesh Sir?'

'Yes.'

'Ma'am, we have to decide about *The Grass* too. When can I ask Ashutosh to send the complete manuscript?'

'You can call for the manuscript. That's not a problem. Let me talk to Aneesh. We're meeting today.'

'Right, ma'am,' Ayesha said and got up.

'Ayesha … There's bad news. Rahul Mehra has disappeared,' Sheela confided to the young girl on a sudden impulse.

Ayesha just stood dumbfounded; she didn't know what to say. She silently came out of Sheela's cabin.

Chapter – 29

The police commissioner of Delhi was under immense pressure from the MEA to solve the case. He had alerted all police stations and directions were given to form special teams. The police commissioner had contacted the police of the neighbouring states as well. A photograph of Rahul Mehra was taken from the camera installed at the MEA's entrance; Rahul had visited the MEA twice so getting his photograph didn't pose any problem. It was sent to the neighbouring states post-haste. The police commissioner was explained as to why this man, who had gone missing, was so important.

******

Even though Ayesha had never met Rahul in person, she was quiet and subdued the entire day, ever since she heard of his disappearance. She kept thinking that it was she who had got Rahul's contact details which were then passed on to Aneesh Nair. What could have happened? According to Ashutosh, the Americans wanted to contact Rahul, who was an ex-chief of the NCB, in connection with some old case in which an American citizen was involved. She prayed that Rahul be found unharmed.

******

Aneesh slipped out of his formal shirt and trousers and put on his pajamas and its matching shirt. It was obvious that he would be spending the night at Sheela's residence. After finishing their dinner, both Aneesh and Sheela sat down in the living room.

Chapter 31

'You were to tell me. What happened to Rahul Mehra?'

'I don't know, Sheela,' Aneesh began, sounding despondent. 'He's not been seen from Tuesday morning. We had deputed two security personnel to keep a watch on him and they had last seen him leaving the apartment for his morning walk. He never returned. One week has passed.'

'What could have happened to him, Aneesh?' She too was disturbed at Rahul's disappearance.

'No idea. I hope he's all right, wherever he is.'

'But you had met him and you might have informed him of the intentions of the Americans.'

'Yes, true, but he was otherwise aware of it. He's an intelligent and matured person.'

'Paul Johnson was said to be involved in narcotics. What I've heard is that these people are dangerous. If Paul Johnson got a hint about the intentions of the American agents, Paul Johnson may harm Rahul Mehra,' Sheela voiced her fears aloud.

'That's exactly what I'm worried about.'

'Was he actually in possession of any evidence?'

'Not as far as I know. The American agents were able to retrieve an email, which contained some documents relating to that old case. But those documents cannot cause any harm to Paul Johnson.'

'That's what you know; Paul Johnson wouldn't know whether the documents are there and if these are there, whether the same are harmful or not,' Sheela reasoned sombrely.

Aneesh kept quiet. This entire matter had become a delicate situation now.

******

Last Tuesday night, a person of Indian origin arrived at Washington D.C. airport. He had an American passport. He scanned the passport at an immigration kiosk and took a small printout. He placed that printout in the passport and produced it before the immigration officer. The officer looked at the photograph, then looked at the face of the person and stamped the passport. He came out of immigration and stopped at the baggage collection area. As soon as he came down the escalator, two Americans approached him, spoke to him for a while and escorted him out of the airport building. He was made to sit in a cab, which drove to a hotel in Arlington. Arlington is a county near Washington D.C. and the drive didn't take more than half an hour. Once they entered the lobby of the hotel, one of the two Americans went to the reception counter, took the key of Room No. 711. Both of them accompanied the man to Room No. 711 located on the sixth floor. They opened the door, again exchanged words with the visitor for a while and left the hotel. The person closed the door and glanced at the mirror just next to the door. The person was Rahul Mehra.

Rahul walked to the window and gazed outside. It was a beautiful view. He kept standing for a while. There was a knock on the door. Rahul opened it. A hotel boy entered, carrying some tea and a few grilled vegetable sandwiches. Rahul really needed both: the tea and something to eat as he was tired and ravenous. When the boy left, he eagerly fell upon the sandwiches. Thereafter, he poured out tea into the cup, added some sugar cubes and a little milk. He stirred it absent-mindedly for awhile, and as he took the first sip, savouring its flavour, he thought of Aneesh Nair in India. He recollected the sequence of events.

*****

Chapter 31

On Sunday, Rahul gave a missed call to Justin. A carrier came within forty minutes. He had already written a small message and placed the same in an envelope. He handed it over to the carrier. The message was:

How can I meet your chief?

In another two hours, the carrier was back with an envelope. Rahul opened it. It was from Justin.

On Tuesday, meet at IGI Airport departure area, Gate No. 6 at 8 a.m. Come prepared to meet the chief. You may have to depart from there. No need to bring anything. Arranging for passport and travel documents. Will be delivered on the spot.

Destroy This Note.

Subsequently, Rahul had reached as per schedule. Justin met him at the airport and gave him an envelope. He simply told him that the documents and the details were in the envelope. Justin got into a waiting car and left.

Rahul opened the envelope. It had an American passport with a different name and a ticket from Delhi to Washington D.C. The flight was to depart at 11.45 a.m. that day. The envelope also contained twenty notes, each of US$100. There was a small note.

Please reach Washington D.C. After clearing immigration, you'll be contacted by our staff. They've made all arrangements that you may require after landing. A small amount of cash is enclosed for your expenses.

Destroy This Note.

Rahul was in jeans and a shirt. While leaving his house, he had placed the pen drive in his pocket. He went inside the airport; he wasn't carrying any luggage with him. His was a business class ticket, which he noticed only at the time of checking-in. He took the boarding pass, got through immigration and security check. He reached the transit hall. There were a lot of shops in that section. He bought a small handbag for his passport and the two books that he bought at an airport shop. There was a layover at Frankfurt airport for two hours and ten minutes. The next flight to Washington D.C. was for nine hours. He had a comfortable journey, being a business class passenger.

******

He finished his tea, and lay down for some time. After a while, when he checked out his room, he found two pairs of jeans and a couple of shirts in the cupboard. He freshened up and changed into the new clothes that had been kept for him in the cupboard. He had been told by the two men who had received him at the airport that they would be back in the evening. At about 5 p.m., he got a call from the reception that he had visitors waiting for him. When he went down, he found those two Americans were waiting for him at the hotel lobby. Rahul was taken to Steve's place. When he got down from the car, two guards escorted him inside the building.

Steve, as usual, was sitting in his usual chair; an adjoining table with a desktop was next to him. Rahul looked at him. Steve was much older than him. Steve didn't get up from the chair and signalled Rahul to sit in the chair, which had been placed for him. Rahul sat down.

'Good evening, Mr Mehra.' Steve was the first one to speak.

'Good evening, sir.'

'It's a pleasure meeting you in person.'

'Thank you, sir, same here.'

'Justin has been in touch with you.'

'Yes, sir.'

Chapter 31

'He was quite appreciative of your help.'

'It was nice of him,' Rahul acknowledged.

'So, were you able to find the pen drive?'

Steve asked a straight question. Rahul was surprised because he had never spoken about the pen drive to Justin.

'Yes, sir.'

'May I have a look?'

Rahul took out a small plastic pouch from his pocket and handed it over to Steve. Steve took out the pen drive, leant forward and attached it to the desktop. There was a screen on the opposite wall. Steve went through the pen drive contents for two hours. He noticed even the minutest of things. At some places, he asked Rahul about some of the drugs, the names of which was unheard of. Rahul told him about the salt of the drug, its effects, side-effects and the places where these were manufactured. Steve also stopped at the trail mail where the complete name of Paul Johnson was mentioned. Once done, he switched off the computer and sat quietly for a while, perhaps reflecting on all that he had seen just now.

He looked at Rahul and said, 'It must have been very difficult for you to close the case, particularly when you had all the details of Paul Johnson's distribution network.'

Rahul simply nodded.

'This is what you wanted to show me?' Steve confirmed.

'This is what you wanted?' Rahul said.

'Yes. Thank you.'

'Will this serve your purpose?'

'I think yes. We couldn't have expected anything better than this.'

'How will you use it to stop Paul Johnson?'

Steve kept quiet. He was tapping the arms of the chair with his forefinger.

'I can give it to the DEA – Drug Enforcement Administration – but what I want is that Paul Johnson should remain in the race for the presidential election. I don't want him to withdraw. Moreover, in the history of the US presidential elections, no nominee has ever withdrawn. I don't want him to make history.'

'How does it matter? What you want is that a person involved in the drug trade shouldn't become the president. Even if he withdraws, he wouldn't be a candidate for the election.'

Steve smiled and said, 'If he withdraws, he'll become more dangerous. He'll try his best so that the replacement candidate wins the election.' Steve paused and then said thoughtfully, 'No, he'll have to contest and lose.'

Rahul remained silent.

Studying him for a moment, Steve asked him, 'Do you want to say something?'

'Don't you wish to know why I took all the trouble and risk to come to you all the way from India?'

'I know the reason. And that's why I was sure that you would cooperate. I really appreciate your courage, Mr Mehra. There are very few brave people like you left in the world.'

Rahul was surprised. He asked, 'Do you really know the reason?'

Steve smiled and said, 'Look, there're still a little more than two months left. We've intelligence that Paul Johnson is aware that we're after him and that we had contacted you. As per our inputs, he has talked to Samuel Garcia. I needn't tell you how dangerous these people are. He may send someone after you. The hotel you're staying in is a sort of our safe house. I suggest you stay here till the elections are over. You're secure here. Once the elections are over, no one is going to look for you.'

Rahul remarked, 'Two months is a pretty long time.'

Chapter 31

'Oh, you're a retired officer, Mr Mehra. Take these two months as a vacation. You're free to move around anywhere. Just inform the reception and everything will be taken care of.'

'Okay, sir. Thank you for the suggestion.'

'Mr Mehra, I'm serious. These people don't think twice before bumping off anyone. Enjoy your stay here as if you're holidaying.'

Rahul stood up, slightly inclined his head and came out. He was escorted back to the hotel in Arlington.

******

Rahul had been staying in the hotel for the last one week. A person might feel lonely but Rahul was used to living alone. He kept watching the news channels. So far, it seemed that Steve hadn't made up his mind to use the evidence against Paul. The opinion polls were predicting that Paul would win the election.

Chapter – 30

Bob Wilson was the administrator of the DEA in the USA. He was sitting with Steve and had just seen the contents of the pen drive received from Rahul Mehra.

Steve said, 'What do you say, Bob? It's your line of expertise.'

'It would have been better if we had this with us prior to the filing of nominations. An action could have definitely been taken and the consequences would have been serious for Paul.'

'Now, at this stage, is something possible? The folder has all the details of the distribution network. Raids can be conducted.'

There was silence as Bob contemplated the possibilities at hand. Looking at Steve, he answered carefully, 'No. It isn't advisable at this stage. It would attract a lot of attention. Do you want me to prepare the grounds for Paul's arrest?'

'No,' Steve said.

'From our angle, once we initiate, things would be unstoppable. We've got to be careful.'

Steve leant back and started tapping the arm of the chair and finally said, 'Okay. Let me see, what else is possible.'

Steve and Bob were old friends; though the latter was much younger, they had known each other for more than a decade.

'What do you have in mind?' Bob asked.

Steve shrugged and said, 'I can't say. I know he should be in prison. I can compel him to withdraw. What I have in mind is that Paul should contest but shouldn't win. I have to reverse public opinion.'

Chapter 31

'This can be done by Sarah. She's the opponent, she has to be more vocal.'

'The problem with her is that she is unlike a politician. She's not interested in negative campaigning.'

'But there may be other politicians in her party, the members of the House of Representatives, who can exploit this information that you have,' Bob suggested.

'You're right. I'll think over it.'

When Bob left, Steve was still in deep thought. He had never failed to get his man in his entire career.

******

Peter Avilov was almost sure that now there was no stopping Paul from becoming the president of the USA. Only two months were left; the public was favouring him. Some shift in the voters' percentage had been seen in the last month but with the news of Rahul's disappearance, it seemed that there wasn't any possibility of American agents laying hands on any evidence against Paul. He still had a stray thought at the back of his mind, a sort of intuition, whether Rahul had been taken over by the CIA. He had, of course, asked Russian intelligence to find out the reason behind Rahul's disappearance. At times, a doubt would creep in that Steve might hit bullseye at the last moment. Peter was also in touch with Aneesh; he was getting regular updates from him. More than fifteen days had passed and people were still in the dark about Rahul's whereabouts.

******

Ayesha had received the complete manuscript from Ashutosh and had reviewed it from the editing angle. It was part of her job. She looked at her watch. It was 3 p.m. She went to Sheela's cabin and found her all by herself. Ayesha closed the door, pulled up a chair and sat down.

Engrossed in her thoughts, Sheela hadn't noticed that Ayesha had come in.

'Good afternoon, ma'am,' Ayesha said, after some time.

'Oh, hello,' Sheela started and then looked at her enquiringly.

'Ma'am, I've gone through the manuscript of *The Grass* and have also done some amount of editing, which I felt was still necessary. I thought I should tell you.'

'Yes, yes. We had discussed this about a week back.'

'Shall I send it for printing? You had said you'll discuss it with Aneesh Sir and tell me what to do.'

'Ayesha, I couldn't talk to him about this. Aneesh is worried about Rahul Mehra. Do you know, fifteen days have passed, and still there's no news?'

'I'll keep the book on hold, then.'

'Yes, I think that will be better.'

'Ma'am, what I can't decide is whether we should retain Chapter 31 or not. Because the novel is complete in all respect at the end of Chapter 30.'

Sheela kept looking at Ayesha, as if staring ahead blankly. After a while, she said, 'Ayesha, that's exactly what has to be decided. Deleting Chapter 31 now, at this stage, will not be appropriate. It has already sold one million copies with thirty-one chapters. Removing the last chapter now, would mean we are not doing justice to the book.'

Ayesha got up and said, 'Okay, ma'am. I'm keeping it on hold.'

As she left the cabin, Sheela felt Ayesha was not her usual bubbly self.

******

Rahul eventually grew tired of watching news channels. Steve hadn't taken any action. Hardly two months were left. He wanted to know what was happening. There was a

Chapter 31

light knock on the door. Rahul opened the door, expecting a housekeeping staff. But surprise, surprise! It was Justin.

'Hello,' Justin greeted him, grinning. He closed the door behind him.

'Hello, are you back?'

'Yes, finally,' Justin said cheerfully as he sat down.

'What's happening?' Rahul asked him eagerly.

'I don't know. I haven't met Steve yet.'

'But there are barely two months left. Don't you think it's high time Steve took some steps?'

'Yes. I'm told there was enough input in that pen drive.'

'He opened it when I was with him. It took two hours to go through the information.'

'I'm sure Steve has something up his sleeve.'

'Justin, I'm getting fed up! This feels like home arrest.'

Justin laughed and said, 'No, not at all. You're free to move. Your name is different. Only one person has seen your face. He's Paul Johnson and even he may not be able to recognize you after so many years. You can't expect him to personally look for you.'

'I want to go back to India, Justin.'

'Are you serious?'

'Yes, of course.'

'I'm told it's for your own safety that you should remain here. If you're really serious, you can return. It's your decision, Mr Mehra. But you would be putting your life in danger.'

'I know, I know.'

'Don't worry, I'm back. I'll keep you company.'

'But what's happening?'

'Wait and watch,' Justin told him cheerfully. 'I'm meeting Steve tonight.'

'Okay.'

Justin warmly shook hands with him and left.

Chapter – 31

It was 5th October. At 9 p.m., BBC London announced a breaking news. The newsreader informed viewers that their undercover reporter had got hold of some sensational documents relating to Paul Johnson, the Republican Party candidate for the post of the president of the USA. The newsreader showed the emails and trail mails pertaining to the supply of drugs throughout the world. The undercover reporter was explaining in detail about the senders, the recipients and the contents of the emails. The reporter's face wasn't shown on TV. Paul Johnson's name was repeatedly mentioned by the reporter. It wasn't revealed from where the emails had been obtained. When the newsreader asked the reporter this, the only answer was that the details had been obtained from a reliable source.

After presenting this news, the newsreader had a detailed discussion with a retired drug enforcement officer, who spoke about the various drug mafias operating, their network, their powerful friends and the secrecy maintained by them. According to him, these documents that showed correspondence within the network were significant from the point of view that it was perhaps a major lapse in the network of the drug mafia.

That breaking news wasn't seen by a majority of Americans at that time because they weren't much used to watching the BBC. The other news channels all over the world gradually started picking up the same story with some additional commentary. It eventually reached American news channels. Fox was the first one.

Next day, when the New York Stock Exchange opened for trading, the stock market crashed. It was a major crash in

Chapter 31

one day. The London Stock Exchange and the Hong Kong Stock Exchange followed suit.

******

Steve had been keeping a tab over the happenings. He was waiting for the after-effects. He felt no need to call Sarah Baker to brief her; her party representatives were there to take care of this. He was confident that this revelation would swing the current public opinion.

******

Rahul, sitting in his hotel room, watched the news. The crash of the New York Stock Exchange would definitely make an impact. He appreciated Steve's decision of leaking the news through the BBC, and not some news channel in the US. The breaking news of the drug trade through an undercover agent was a brilliant idea. Rahul had observed that only selective emails had been shown. The systematic analysis of news by some of the experts was sufficient to impact the poll prospects.

******

Aneesh Nair, in Delhi, had seen the news. It was big news. A candidate for the presidentship of the USA was being accused of being a drug trader. He too was minutely following the emails, which were being shown on various news channels. He recollected some of the paragraphs of Ajeet Singh's statement. Ajeet Singh had been confronted with the emails on the laptop. Though there wasn't any reference to any specific email in the said statement, it looked obvious to Aneesh that the folders and documents in the laptop had been handed over to a BBC reporter. These details could have been made available only by Rahul. The pen drive, which Rahul had misplaced seemed to have been found, and thereafter found its way into the hands of the CIA. After pondering on this issue for some time, Aneesh gradually came to the conclusion that if the details had been taken from that pen drive, then Rahul was alive, living somewhere and unharmed. That was a huge consolation. His mobile rang. It was Peter.

'Hello?' came Peter's voice.

'Hello.'

'Aneesh, you might have seen the news and the fallout.'

'Yes, I've seen it.'

'Rahul is the man behind all this!'

'One cannot say with surety, Peter.'

'The CIA had been pursuing him relentlessly for the evidence. I'm sure it's the CIA who has done this. Have you found out anything about Rahul Mehra?'

'No, he's still missing.'

'There was a commitment and we were assured that Rahul Mehra wouldn't hand over any evidence to the American agent,' Peter rebuked.

'Yes,' Aneesh replied calmly. 'There was a commitment. I'm still sure it's not Rahul who is behind all this. The CIA has a number of sources. But then, who knows, it's our presumption. There's a possibility that the undercover reporter of BBC had been working separately on this for quite some time. You know, there are a lot of journalists who are ready to risk their life to go to that extent.'

'That possibility cannot be ruled out but my mind goes back to Rahul Mehra again and again.'

'Look, it's not necessary at this stage to analyse what could be the source of BBC's news. What is important is to analyse the fallout,' Aneesh reasoned.

'The fallout is obvious. A big chunk of voters is going to switch over to the Sarah Baker camp. We're trying to control the damage,' Peter sounded extremely perturbed, which wasn't surprising.

Chapter 31

'Peter, the Indian government will always be with you. We support your policies.'

'Yes, but this time, the fallout is going to be costly. Anyway, please keep me updated if you get any information about that ex-chief.'

Aneesh assured him that he would and they disconnected.

******

Paul was dumbfounded. The news and the fallout came as a shock. He kept avoiding the press and the media. The Republican Party members of the senate had directed Paul to clarify his position. That had happened the first time. Paul's election managers had been looking at Paul for the last two days, hoping that he might come forward with something to disprove the allegations. It had become an exceedingly difficult task for both of them to handle the media personnel. Finally, on the third day, a press release was issued by Paul, which read:

> *Never in the history of America has the campaigning for presidential election touched such a low point. Never in the history of America has any candidate for the post of president been maligned thus. This is disgraceful. Two news articles had appeared earlier, linking my name with some drug trader. Let me clarify in categorical terms, I've no links with any drug trader. It's unfortunate that I have to give such a clarification. The two separate articles, which had appeared earlier, were regarded as rumours, which, sometimes, are created during the course of campaigning; I never thought those to be important. Giving importance to such rumours was unnecessary, I had felt. I had ignored those.*
>
> *Now, two days back, the BBC, a reputed news channel of the United Kingdom, has made allegations based on a source – a so-called undercover agent. The undercover*

agent hasn't come forward. The purported emails have made an attempt to link my name. Any intelligent person can read between the lines. Why was such breaking news been given in another country? It was sensational news! But was it news? No. It was fake, with false, created emails. Even the email address isn't mine. An attempt has been made in a big way to malign me, your Republican candidate, to put me on the defensive.

If the opponent party or its candidate have anything against me, place it before the DEA. Let them investigate. But no such evidence has ever been brought on record simply because there is no evidence. I have no relationship with any drug mafia. It is only malicious campaigning. It's a conspiracy to defame your candidate. I would say that the origin of such conspiracy is not in America. Americans do not utilize their brain in such a degrading manner. They do not believe in negativity. The source of such conspiracy may be Russian intelligence, who do not want to see your favourite candidate as the next president of America. The Russians are afraid that once I become president, they will have to face more tariff restrictions. They are afraid there will be sanctions, that there will be much more expenditure towards defence. They are afraid that America's influence over Afghanistan, Syria, Pakistan, Iraq and other countries will increase.

This is a big conspiracy to defeat your favourite candidate, my fellow citizens. This is not an attack on me. This is not an attack on Republicans. This is an attack on you, the citizens of America. I request you, don't fall into the trap. Don't believe the fake news. Don't believe the rumours. Show them that you're strong and cannot be misled by any outside forces.

The above statement in the shape of a press release by Paul was flashed on news channels. And, it had the desired impact. The rider in the press release that Russian intelligence was conspiring was a well-thought-up strategy. The Americans wouldn't like Russian interference.

Chapter 31

When campaigning had started, the percentage of public opinion in favour of Paul was sixty-three, and thirty-seven in favour of Sarah. The two earlier news articles had resulted in a slight shift and the ratio became 60:40, sixty in favour of Paul. The impact of the stock markets' crash had been huge. The ratio shifted to 40:60, with sixty in favour of Sarah. With the issuance of the press release, there was some swing back. The ratio became 45:55, fifty-five in favour of Sarah. Poll experts were discussing on various channels that Paul could still make it. The margin could be reduced. There was, however, less than a month left now. The members of the senate of the Republican Party had personally come forward. They started conducting small meetings. They would explain on one-to-one communication as to how the Russians were bent on destroying the poll prospects of Paul Johnson.

******

Donald Chen had seen the statement made by Paul and was confused. He had been told that the Russians were the major fundraisers in Super PACs, supporting Paul's campaigns whereas Paul was accusing the Russians of meddling in the American election campaign in order to ensure his defeat! He wanted to meet Paul but now it seemed practically impossible. Paul became inaccessible.

******

Peter had also seen Paul's statement. It was a smart move. He smiled at the notion of 'Russians conspiring to defeat Paul Johnson.' He was wondering how he could use this part of Paul's statement to their advantage. He was keeping an eye on the opinion polls. At present, Paul was seemingly on the losing side. Some efforts might be needed to get back to his earlier ratings.

In another ten days, the efforts of the Republican Party members brought favourable results. The margin had reduced. The public debates and opinions brought the ratio to 48:52, forty-eight in favour of Paul and fifty-two in favour of Sarah. It became a closely contested election, which at one time had been one-sided. There were still twenty days left.

Smelling victory, the members of the Democratic Party swung into action. They started criticizing the press release. For the first time, they openly came forward, stating that Paul Johnson was in nexus with a drug trader of Columbia. They made placards, with one stating:

WE DO NOT WANT A DRUG TRADER TO BE OUR PRESIDENT

Another one stated:

SAVE AMERICA FROM A DRUG MAFIA

It became an open war of words.

Chapter – 32

A passenger was intercepted at London's Heathrow Airport. He was bound for Moscow on a KLM flight. He was drunk and began misbehaving with the immigration officers when he was asked to show his passport. He was taken to a separate room so that the other passengers in the queue wouldn't be inconvenienced. He was found to be of Russian origin but a citizen of the UK. When he continued to misbehave, the KLM officials handed him over to the local police. He was brought to the police headquarters for further investigation. On questioning, he was found to be giving incoherent answers. He was detained overnight.

Next day, when he seemed normal, he was again questioned. His handbag was examined. It was found to contain a folder, which had a bunch of printouts, showing correspondence through emails. After going through these, it was found that these were the copies of emails relating to Paul Johnson that had been broadcasted by the BBC. When asked about the same, he stated that he worked in a software company and that he had not only cooked up these emails but had also handed over the same to the undercover reporter of the BBC. The police officials found that he wasn't in a normal state of mind. They allowed him to go. But this sequence of events was uploaded on the social media by someone and it went viral. This post was brought to the attention of Paul's election managers, who in turn showed it to Paul. Immediately, a small statement was drafted. It read:

> *A gentleman in London has claimed that he cooked up the email correspondences and handed them over to the BBC reporter. We do not know the authenticity of his claim. This, however, strengthens our stand that whatever was shown on BBC was 'fake news'.*

The Republican Party members seized the opportunity and started campaigning vigorously, shouting from the rooftops that the Russians were responsible for spreading such misinformation. Public opinion now stood at 50:50 in most of the opinion polls. Only ten days were left.

Steve called Bob Wilson again.

'Look, sir, it has become a close contest now,' Bob said, as he sat down opposite Steve.

'Yes, Bob, but I don't want to take any chances. I was hoping that the shift of voting percentage at 60:40 in favour of Sarah would continue. Paul and his party are really working hard. They've managed to bring the percentage at par. It could be anybody's game.'

'That's right.'

'I want your help.'

'Yes, sir. Please tell me, how can I help you?'

'I'm told that the DEA has an office in Thailand.'

'Yes, the DEA has offices in Bangkok, Chiang Mai and Udorn in Thailand. We have a regional director posted at Bangkok. That office looks after operations in thirty-four countries of Southeast Asia.'

'Does the Royal Thai Police work for you?'

'Let's not say they work for us, but yes, they do act upon our information and suggestions.'

Steve picked up a piece of paper and passed it to Bob.

'Here are four addresses in Thailand. These have been taken from a folder, which was found in one of the laptops. These four appear to work on a large scale, and were part of Paul Johnson's network. I'm not aware of their current position. Pass these addresses to your regional office. Let them pick up any two out of these four. Get them searched. Hopefully, you may get something. The names of the individuals are also given. Detain those individuals and get their statements recorded. I needn't tell you that I want the name of Paul Johnson specifically to be mentioned. That they were or are, whatever, working for him.'

Chapter 31

Bob studied the sheet and then looked at him.

'Sir, are you sure we'll find them still in operation? The list you have is ten years old.'

'Let's hope for the best, Bob. Once you get into the drug trade, it's impossible to come out of it.'

'When do you want this done?'

'Immediately.'

'It'll be done.' Bob nodded as he got up and left.

Next day, raids were conducted at two places, both in Chiang Mai. The persons were found to be operating under the garb of tourist offices. Their statements were recorded. The names of Paul Johnson and Samuel Garcia were made to be written. All individuals were also detained for further scrutiny.

Not only was wide publicity of the busting of the drug racket given in the local press, the chief of the Royal Thai Police appeared on news channels and gave interviews.

This happened nine days before the US presidential election.

All these news clippings and TV interviews were sufficient fodder for the Democrats to be used in the coming days.

******

Rahul was noting all these developments with great interest. The unfolding of events had become much like the well-written manuscript of a thriller, and suspense was looming large. Who would be the next president?

******

The day of electing the next president came in due course. The voting was always done on a predetermined day, and passed off peacefully. Rahul rang up Justin.

'Hello, Justin?' Rahul said.

'Hello sir, the wait is over.'

'Yes, thankfully! Now you can book my ticket to India. I'm in captivity here,' Rahul said jokingly.

'Sir, please don't use the word captivity. In fact, I was about to call you. Steve wants to meet you tomorrow morning.'

'What now?'

'Maybe, it's a thanksgiving. Sir, I'll come and pick you up at 9 a.m. Does that suit you?'

'Yes, sure.'

Next morning, Justin and Rahul entered Steve's living room. Steve was not alone; there was a lady sitting with him. She was Sarah Baker. Rahul had seen her face on TV channels numerous times in recent days. Steve extended his hand and gripped Rahul's hand. It was a strong grip and he shook Rahul's hand warmly.

Steve said, 'Mr Mehra, meet our next president, Mrs Sarah Baker.'

Rahul shook hands with Sarah and sat down. Justin too took a seat.

'Are you confident about Mrs Baker winning the elections, sir?' Rahul enquired.

'It's your prediction, sir,' Sarah Baker chipped in.

'I'm confident Paul will lose the election.'

'Mrs Baker, this gentleman here, Rahul Mehra, would be the reason for your win. He has displayed extreme courage and patience while helping us,' Steve said, grinning. He next addressed Justin and said, 'Justin, can you please arrange tea for everybody? Let us have the privilege of having a cup of tea with this beautiful lady, who is going to be our president.'

Smiling, Justin nodded and went out; Sarah almost blushed.

Chapter 31

'You're very kind, sir. I'm obliged,' Rahul acknowledged, inclining his head slightly.

'You're wrong, Mr Mehra. *We* are obliged. Tell me, Mr Mehra, have you heard of the movie *Argo*?'

'No, I haven't, sir.'

Steve was about to speak when Justin entered with a tray carrying cookies, four tea cups and a teapot.

Steve stood up to help Justin place the tray in front of them, and poured out tea for everyone. As they all settled down with their tea and cookies, Steve narrated the storyline of *Argo* to Rahul.

'It is based on a true incident. One of our operatives, Tony Mendez, went to Tehran to rescue six American diplomats, who had taken refuge in the Canadian embassy while others were taken as hostages. Tony was our ex-filtration specialist. He met those six Americans, provided each with a Canadian passport and brought them back safe and sound on a Swissair flight. In order to protect the remaining hostages in Tehran, our involvement was suppressed and credit was given to the Canadian government.'

All were listening with rapt attention as they had their tea. Steve continued, 'Tony was awarded the Intelligence Star at a ceremony. The movie ends here.'

They all kept quiet. Steve further said, 'Do you know how many persons were present at the award ceremony?'

'How many?' Rahul asked.

'Two: the president and Tony.'

'That's great, sir. You wanted to ensure that his involvement remained a secret.'

'At that point of time, yes.'

As they finished their tea, Steve said, 'Mr Mehra, I told you the above incident just to emphasize that you are Tony Mendez for us. No one will ever know what you've done for our county.'

'You're right, sir. I must congratulate Mr Mehra for going out of his way to help us.' Sarah Baker turned to face Rahul, and said gratefully, 'Thank you, sir. We'll never forget what you've done for our country.'

Rahul addressed them both, choosing his words carefully so as not to sound offensive, 'Very respectfully, I'll submit that I didn't take the trouble to come here to become Tony Mendez. There was another reason.'

Steve looked at him and said, 'Mr Mehra, you never wanted that our country should meet the same fate as your country. Isn't that the reason?'

'Yes.'

'I knew all along that he became the ...'

They all remained silent for a few minutes. Steve said, 'You are no more in danger. I don't think you need any security because from now onwards you're no longer important to either Paul or the Russians. You know that. Justin will accompany you to Delhi and he'll be there till the next president is officially sworn-in.'

'Thank you, sir, and thank you, ma'am,' Rahul smiled, slightly inclining his head. They all shook hands warmly, and Justin and Rahul left for the hotel.

******

Justin booked tickets for both of them to Delhi the same night. The following day, when they arrived at Delhi airport, it was night-time. Rahul hired a cab from the airport, and was back at his apartment around midnight. The guard sitting on the ground floor, stared at him incomprehensibly. He couldn't believe Rahul Mehra was back alive, and unharmed, after such a long time. Rahul opened the door to his apartment and turned back to see that the door of the next apartment was locked and there was no camera. He entered his apartment, switched on the light and looked around. Everything was intact.

Chapter 31

Rahul woke up a bit late the next morning. He looked at his watch; it was 9 a.m. The first thing he did was to charge his phone as it had been switched off for almost three months. Next, he prepared a cup of green tea. Sipping it, he scouted around to see what all provisions he would have to buy, now that he was back home for good. He thought of going to the market downstairs to buy some grocery and other necessities such as milk. While having his tea, he switched on his laptop which he had left back at his home. The details of the pen drive were copied therein. He scanned the same and smiled to himself. By the time it was 12.15 p.m., he had got his house cleaned which had been locked all these several weeks, and had arranged for grocery and other necessary provisions. At 12.30 p.m., he decided to call Aneesh.

'Hello?' Aneesh spoke softly at the other end.

'Hello,' Rahul responded.

Aneesh froze; he recognized the voice. He looked at his mobile screen to be certain. Yes, it was Rahul Mehra.

'Oh God! How are you, sir? Where were you? How have you been?' The questions poured out like a torrent from Aneesh.

'Can we meet, Mr Nair?'

'Yes, yes.'

'Will you send me an official vehicle one more time?'

'Sir, please meet me somewhere outside. Not at my office.'

'Suggest the place.'

'At 1.30 p.m.? Let's have lunch together. We can meet at Constitution Club. There's a good place to sit there.'

'I'll be there at 1.30,' Rahul assured him and disconnected.

Aneesh was in a state of shock. All the negativity in his mind had disappeared. So, Rahul was back, he heaved a sigh of relief. It felt really good to hear his voice. After twenty minutes, when he was preparing to leave, his phone rang. It was Sheela. He answered the call.

'Hello!'

Sheela was struck by the ring of joviality in Aneesh's voice.

'Hey, what happened? You're sounding cheerful!'

'Sheela,' the excitement in Aneesh's voice was palpable, 'Rahul Mehra is back! He just called me. I'm going to have lunch with him.'

'Oh, that's good news! May I join you? I'd like to meet him.'

Aneesh thought for a moment and finally said, 'No, not this time. I've a lot to hear from him. I'll invite him some other time.'

'Okay.'

'You called – is there something you wanted to talk about?'

'I just wanted to hear your voice, silly man!'

'So sweet,' chuckled Aneesh. 'I'll call back soon ... cheerio!'

Chapter – 33

They met at the Constitution Club.

Aneesh gripped Rahul's hand firmly and said, 'Perhaps you haven't any idea how very happy I am to see you after such a long time.'

'Thank you, Mr Nair. I feel the same way.'

'You know, I made all efforts to find you after you disappeared. It was so sudden. I kept getting all kinds of negative thoughts. I wished all the time that you should be well, wherever you were. By the way, where were you all this time?'

Rahul looked at Aneesh. There was sincerity in what Aneesh had said. Rahul could understand that Aneesh's reaction was spontaneous.

'I was able to locate the pen drive. I saw the contents,' replied Rahul, as they sat down at a table.

'Mr Mehra, you'd promised that you'll tell me if you found the pen drive.'

'Yes, I did promise. I was in three minds at that time. First was to give it to you; second was to give it to Justin Brown; and third was to keep mum. It was a difficult decision.'

'But then you decided to give it to the Americans, the CIA?'

'That's right.'

'And I was thinking that you would cooperate with us – I mean the Indian government. You'd been a loyal employee of the government.'

Rahul chose to ignore the comment.

'You were, perhaps, following the news, particularly the one relating to the US presidential election,' Rahul said.

'Yes, I saw that the BBC broadcasted the details of the email correspondence. I could gather that these must be from you because there was a reference to that email in one of the documents that you'd given me.'

'You might be the only one to guess that.'

'Peter Avilov, the Russian diplomat I've been in contact with, had called. He was suspicious but I convinced him that it couldn't have come from you.'

'So, he did call you?'

'Yes,' Aneesh said, 'as a matter of fact, he enquired about you twice. First, when you'd disappeared and again when the BBC broadcasted the details of the emails. I told him to concentrate on the fallout of those emails and forget about you. There was a swing in the public opinion after that report by the BBC.'

'Yes, there was.'

'So, what do you think, Mr Mehra? Will Sarah Baker win?'

'They're equally poised.'

'How did it all happen? Where had you actually gone?' Aneesh couldn't contain his curiosity anymore.

'It's a long story, Mr Nair. I can simply tell you that I was in the USA and I'll not lie to you that I had personally handed over the pen drive to the CIA chief.'

'Did you meet him?'

'Yes.'

'In person?'

'Yes.'

'Searches were conducted in Thailand. Was that also a part of your strategy?'

'Mr Nair, let me clarify one thing. I haven't done anything except hand over the pen drive. When it was to be used and how it was used was their prerogative.'

Chapter 31

In the meantime, their lunch had been served and they had been conversing while having their lunch. The restaurant in the club wasn't much crowded because of limited accessibility.

When they finished lunch, Aneesh said, 'Sir, did it never occur to you that the pen drive should have been given to the Indian government?'

'Yes. It did occur,' replied Rahul tersely, wiping his mouth with his napkin. 'But nobody ever asked me what happened to the minister. You also didn't ask me, the most important question.'

Aneesh gravely looked at Rahul, who was staring at him with an equally grave expression. Very slowly Aneesh said, 'Because I know what happened to that minister.'

'Then you have the answer.'

Rahul stood up, dropped the napkin on the table and left without waiting for Aneesh to get up.

When Aneesh came out of the Constitution Club, he was feeling utterly dejected. He didn't feel like going back to his office. He called Sheela instead.

'Hello, are you busy?'

'What's this about?'

'Are you busy?' Aneesh repeated.

'Not for you.'

'Okay,' Aneesh felt his spirits rising. 'I'm coming right now to pick you up.'

'Where are we going?'

'To your place.'

'Why don't you go there directly, Aneesh? I'll reach home at about the same time too.'

'Okay. Please don't keep me waiting.'

In another half an hour, they were sitting together in Sheela's living room.

'What happened? You're not your usual charming self now,' Sheela said gently.

'Yeah, I'm feeling somewhat dejected.'

'Why? You were meeting Rahul Mehra, weren't you?'

'Yes, I met him. But he made me realize that we, the bureaucrats, are puppets.'

Sheela looked at Aneesh's gloomy face. She went up to him, hugged him and lightly caressed his cheek.

'That's exactly what you never wanted to realize earlier. Don't get depressed. Cheer up. You're a strong man!'

Aneesh looked at Sheela's confidence – a business woman, free, liberal, unscarred, outspoken and contented. Sheela asked Amma to make strong hot coffee for both of them. Sheela knew that the filter coffee prepared by Amma had no match.

While they were having coffee, she asked, 'What did he say, where was he all this while?'

'In the USA,' taking another sip of Amma's coffee.

'Did he go there willingly?'

'Yes, he did help the CIA.'

Sheela took a sip and glancing at him sideways, said, 'I haven't yet given a nod for the printing of *The Grass*.'

'Why?'

'I wanted your confirmation.'

'For what?' Aneesh was astonished.

'Regarding the last chapter. Shall we go ahead with thirty-one chapters?'

Aneesh laughed out heartily and asked, 'Since when have you started taking my advice in your business affairs?'

'This was necessary.'

'What do *you* think?' Aneesh looked at her adoringly.

'We won't do justice to the book if we delete Chapter 31 at this stage.'

Chapter 31

'I totally agree with you. It should be in the market just as it is now.'

They looked at each other affectionately, and when Sheela rested her head on his shoulder, Aneesh wrapped his arms around her, drawing her close to him in a tight embrace.

******

Days passed. The results of the US presidential election were officially declared in the first week of January. Sarah Baker had won by a margin of 1.8 per cent.

Chapter – 34

It was the launching of *The Grass*. About eighty people attended this special occasion, which was held at a small conference hall in the hotel, The Hilton. The event was organized by Spellers, and was routine for them. For almost all books, a book launch was held and it was a part of the marketing of a book. Though *The Grass* had already been a bestseller and didn't require much publicity, Spellers wanted to tell the world that *The Grass* was now one of the products of their publishing house. Moreover, Ashutosh, the author, hadn't participated in the earlier launch, which was said to have been organized by some event management company.

There were about seventeen to eighteen round tables, each being a five-seater. There was no platform or podium in the conference hall. Four chairs were placed as the front row, where a banner with *The Grass* written boldly across it was also prominently displayed. Invitees included journalists from different newspapers, magazines and TV channels. Ashutosh, Sujata, Ayesha, Sanjeev and Shankar were already there supervising the arrangements.

By 8 p.m., most of the guests had taken their seats. At 8 p.m., Sheela Nair entered the conference hall. For the first time, everyone saw Aneesh Nair, her husband, accompanying her. Sheela greeted everyone personally and introduced Aneesh to everyone.

Ayesha asked Ashutosh, Sheela and Shankar to come forward and sit on the chairs placed as the front row. Aneesh, Sujata and Sanjeev sat at one of the tables near the front row. Ayesha had a mic in her hand. She too sat down and requested Sheela to address the audience. Sheela briefly introduced Spellers which included its birth and its journey

Chapter 31

thus far, mentioned some of the past bestsellers published by them and introduced Ashutosh as the author of *The Grass*. Sujata clapped enthusiastically when Ashutosh was introduced.

At that moment, when Sheela had just finished her speech, Rahul entered the conference hall. He stood at the entrance and looked around. Aneesh noticed him. He quickly got up and escorted him to the table where he was sitting. Sheela glanced from the corner of her eyes and correctly guessed that the elderly gentleman would be Rahul Mehra. Ashutosh was given the mic. He spoke a few words. He narrated how he got the inspiration to pen the book. When he finished, he handed the mic back to Ayesha. She had already marked a few paragraphs in the book which she would be reading aloud at the book launch. She read out those paragraphs one by one. These were standard rituals of any book launch. Shankar thereafter announced that anyone who purchased a copy of *The Grass* at the event that evening, could get it autographed by the author, Ashutosh. It took about an hour for the scheduled programme to be over. While Shankar was making the announcement, Sheela came near Aneesh, met Rahul and whispered something to Aneesh. As soon as Shankar finished his announcement, Aneesh stood up and requested the mic from Shankar.

Then, mic in hand, Aneesh addressed the gathering.

'Ladies and gentleman, we have with us this evening a very experienced and learned gentleman, Mr Rahul Mehra. He is not from the literary world and may not be an expert in this field. However, he has vast experience. I will request him to say a few words to all of us at this occasion and enrich us.'

Rahul was taken by surprise. He hadn't expected this. He had come only because of Aneesh's special request.

'Please sir, here is the mic and keep sitting. You are older to all of us,' Aneesh said, handing the mic to Rahul amidst a round of polite applause.

Rahul took the mic. Gathering together his thoughts, he addressed the invitees.

'Really, this is unexpected. I had never thought that I would be asked to speak before such an educated and esteemed audience.' Rahul looked at Aneesh, Sheela, Ayesha, Ashutosh and all those sitting around. His gaze shifted back to Aneesh. He said, 'Thank you, Aneesh, for your kind words about me. To be respected thus is rare these days.' He was silent for a few minutes and then continued.

'As Aneesh has informed you. I've no knowledge of literature. This is a book launch. I'm the odd man out. My link with books is only to the extent that I do read fiction. To be honest, I've no interest in non-fiction. I've read *The Grass*. I found it to be a gripping novel. I came in contact with Ashutosh because of the last chapter, Chapter 31. It looked unusual. It was a sort of misfit. It must have occurred to most of you that the last chapter was unnecessary. I too noticed that. But I quote Mark Twain, who said "Truth is stranger than fiction but it is because fiction is obliged to stick to possibilities. Truth isn't." Fiction is the creation of the human mind and is congenial to it. Fiction has to be possible. Fiction has to make sense. Truth is not required to make sense. You all are well-known critics of books, particularly of fiction. You won't accept any absurdity in the sequence of events.'

Rahul stopped, looked around the hall, particularly at Ashutosh and then at Ayesha. He continued, 'In *The Grass*, Chapter 31 was seemingly a misfit. All of you would have expected the novel to finish at Chapter 30. Anything thereafter looked absurd. It looked the same to me. I have read a great many bestsellers. Those became bestsellers because of a sound plot, good narration and a captivating unfolding of events. But unfortunately, you'll all excuse me, the climax in most of those books wasn't good. Sometimes, I felt as if the author did not know how to take the story to its logical conclusion, while at other times I felt that the author was in a hurry to finish it off.

Chapter 31

'*The Grass*, on the other hand, has a riveting climax. I request all of you to read it. Thank you for listening to me.'

He put the mic on the table. There was a big round of applause. Sheela was delighted. She had always thought that critics, analysts and journalists were the best in such events, but this elderly gentleman had given the true analysis.

Shankar announced that dinner had been served and requested the invitees to proceed to the dining area. Ashutosh was busy signing copies of the book. It was a thrilling occasion for him. After signing the last copy, he came to the table where Rahul, Aneesh, Sheela, Sujata and Ayesha were sitting and chatting.

Rahul congratulated Ashutosh and said, 'You know, there are some other facts that would make the climax of *The Grass* even more engrossing. If I tell you, you could add another chapter – Chapter 32.'

Sheela was quick. She said, 'Sir, please tell us. We'll add it. A climax should be outstanding to make a book a bestseller.'

Rahul lowered his head momentarily, raised it slightly, looked at Aneesh and said, 'But *The Grass* is already a bestseller.'

THE END